Fea
of the
Dead

SOURCE POINT PRESS

Edited by
Parris Young
Trico Lutkins
Brittany Werner
and
Joshua Werner

www.sourcepointpress.com

Printed in the United States of America.
First Printing, 2013 by Source Point Press

ISBN-10: 0989650448
ISBN-13: 978-0-9896504-4-1

www.sourcepointpress.com

www.facebook.com/SourcePointPress

Table of Contents

3

Piper

by Jay Wilburn

It was the rats that beat the humans, but not with bites.
Their fleas carried the venom that killed them those nights.
When the rats were dead, the humans were next.
When the dead rose up, the humans were perplexed.
Worst of all was the hunger they felt.
It caused the corpses to bite and then the infection was dealt.
Fever led to death, but not for long.
Death was replaced by reanimation and moaning for their
song.

****

Piper Hamel flew the Cessna over the battered landscape. She listened to the propellers with pleasure knowing her father would be proud that what he taught her had saved her life.

He had built planes like this his entire life and taught her to fly even though Piper's mother had thought she was far too young.

He would not have been happy with her choice of craft. Mr. Hamel had worked for the Piper company. He named his only child Piper. Cessna was the able enemy. He would not be happy with that at all.

If he was not trying to claw his way out of his coffin to taste the flesh of the living, he would be rolling over in his fresh grave. Piper had no way of knowing this, but what was left of her mother was lying still next to him having died much earlier than the plague.

Mr. Hamel's timing was poor and he was buried before the new rules of death were discovered.

****

4

She almost didn't take up the Cessna when she found it, but they were closing in behind her. They were following her sound, they were fixed on her smell, and they were hungry for her flesh.

Piper had gone back to work immediately after her father's funeral and a few drinks. That's how she got trapped in her studio for the first few months. She quickly exhausted the food in the machines and had to sneak out occasionally for more.

She had learned a few tricks by using her own art that helped her get around the searching dead. It worked fairly well until she made a terrible error in judgment and got surrounded.

She had fled trying to distract them and circle back around, but every noise she made just drew more of them to her and they forced her forward even as she led them along.

That is how she ended up at the private airfield looking at the brightly colored Cessna with very little time to spare.

The plane had a banner attached to the back advertising the *Captain James's Calabash Seafood Buffet and Bar*. She unhooked it from the tail and rushed her preflight check. She pulled the blocks from where they were chocked under the wheels as the dead were pressing through the same hole in the fence she had used. She walked the nose into position slowly as the corpses shuffled through the grass toward the runway.

Piper opened the door on the rainbow painted side that read, *Big John's Advertising*. The engine wouldn't crank at first. The mangled bodies had reached the tarmac and were approaching shoulder to torn shoulder along the narrow runway behind her.

She calmly worked the choke in the deliberate fashion she had been taught. The engine gave a strangled whine as the propellers turned in sleepy circles. The followers in the front of the mob were close enough then for Piper to hear one of them squeaking. If she had turned around, she would have seen the cadaver's vocal cords straining inside his open throat. In her mind, she pictured a tin can with a violin string being drawn slowly through a hole in the center of the can.

She had used that technique once when laying down sound for a horror movie that would never be released now.

The plane taxied forward at a crawl. She pulled the door closed and let the plane build gradually even as the creatures reached out for the rudders. She knew better than to flood the engine in a panic.

She could hear her father's scolding tone. *I don't care if an army of the walking dead is dogging your tail, Ms. Piper Hamel,* he would say, *this craft is not a hotrod. You treat it with respect and care, if you want her to lift you into the sky out of their dead, clutching grasp.*

The plane reached the sweet point and Piper worked the controls to lift the Cessna off the ground. The dead reached out for her as she flew over the trees and left them behind.

She could no longer see them, but they continued forward over the end of the runway and through the grass. Their bodies piled against the fence and bent it forward on the concrete basing buried in the shallow dirt. The blackened earth below the thick grass cracked and belched up under the pressure of their surging weight. The fence did not break, but folded down and their bare feet clattered over the top of it. They continued on in a steady line across the airfield, over the downed fence, and through the trees long after the buzz of the engines had faded on the brittle surface of their dead eardrums.

Back in the plane, Piper had listened to the beautiful hum of the engines as she watched her town burn silently below her.

****

Piper had landed three times to refuel, find food, and to rest. One of those times had gone well. She had to make an escape each time. Two of those three times were because of humans.

She had to find a safe place to land longer than a refueling run or a rest break.

6

In her mind she heard her father's voice, scolding her again. *Ms. Piper Hamel*, he was ranting, *how could you fly through the apocalypse in a Cessna, all pied in rainbow pastels of all things, after I spent my life building perfectly good Pipers by the sweat of my brow? Why are you doing this to me, girl?*

Piper imagined his voice crackling over an old record player or through a horn bell with a microphone in a toilet. She had used that once for a ghost in a horror comedy. She didn't normally do voices, but the production company wanted some background gibberish.

She also imagined adding chains for her father's ghost. She would use the tire chain on the tiled, folly board she kept near her projection screen in her studio.

She had been doing some fairly tame folly work on a cartoon about aliens before the creatures interrupted her recording and destroyed the world.

Her father considered her job one step above playing dress up in her old bedroom back home. He liked to listen to her tell stories about how she created various sounds, but he always footnoted her stories with some comment about real work.

She pulled out of her thoughts when the engines stuttered before roaring back up to full speed again. Piper sighed and scanned the ground below for a clear path where she could land and either search for fuel or flee for cover.

She needed to find something or she was coming down hard.

****

Her engines were thirsty and dry.
She dropped into Haven from the sky.
The dead surrounded the walls;
The living cowered in their halls.
She was in time for Marty's birthday party,
But alas the supplies were not hearty.
She needed to make a trade.

7

So a deal with all Haven she made.

****

Piper spotted the wide street partly because the rough triangle of the compound was framed by a thick layer of writhing bodies around the perimeter. She already felt trapped as she imagined coming to rest in the center of that mass. The dead were there because they had been drawn by sounds or they smelled something they wanted to eat. The people might be desperate, trapped, and just as violent as the other groups she had fled. There might not be any fuel inside the triangle either.

As long as she was in the air, she was free from the confines of the fences and the reach of the walking death. She felt tightness around her neck as she banked the plane and viewed the turning triangle below her. She at least knew the creatures had not broken through the perimeter yet.

She was coming down very soon one way or the other. Gliding the Cessna in a controlled crash was not desirable when she might need to run and no ambulances were coming. If she landed outside the triangle, she would have to contend with the dead that surrounded it. If she landed inside, it would at least be a real landing and she would be safe from one threat temporarily.

There was no time left.

She aligned herself with the avenue again once she created the distance she needed for the timed approach. She dropped down smoothly as her wheels soared just over the heads of the bodies. They jostled and jerked as they tried to look up at her on their tight, lifeless neck muscles. She could see their bloodshot sclera in the whites of their eyes for those that still had their eyes.

As she passed just above it, she saw that some form of sheet metal had been used to create the walls of the triangle. The buildings had been part of a small downtown area including gas stations and shops before they were sealed off from the monsters.

There was debris around the inside edges of the walls and scattered around the smaller streets off the main avenue.

She coasted in carefully with her wings centered and level between the buildings on both sides. She bounced slightly as her gear kissed the pavement. She adjusted and came to rest rolling out the momentum before the avenue was cut off by the angle of the opposing, metal wall.

Piper was too close to taxi around for another takeoff. She would have to turn the plane manually and leave the way she had come. There was not going to be a quick retreat, if there was trouble in this trap. She did not have enough fuel left for an escape either.

She cut off the engines and let the propellers wind down into silence.

There was popping and thumping on the other side of the metal wall outside her windshield. She could see the barrier bowing out in dents and retracting again like a living thing.

The walls greatly muffled their voices on the other side. The steady patter like rain on metal and the relative quiet were unnerving to Piper.

She waited.

Two men stepped out into the street slowly from around the far edge of one of the buildings near where she had stopped. One had a rifle the other was carrying the cast iron shaft of a large candelabra.

Piper waited for them to reach the plane. There was nowhere to run and she was out of good options.

They stood at the window. They looked at each other and then back at Piper inside. One of them knocked lightly on her window.

Piper waved at them. They looked at each other and then back at Piper again. Both men raised one hand each and waved back without smiling.

****

9

She walked with them up the deserted avenue. There was a lot of paper lying around the gutters and along the edges of the buildings. Black, trash bags were filled and stacked in corners between buildings. Some windows were boarded and others were partially broken out of their frames.

A couple cars on side streets sat on blocks. The interior sections had been stripped down to the chaises.

The men didn't volunteer any information other than they were taking her to speak to Baker and Butch at the birthday party. Piper didn't ask any questions after that explanation.

They took her up the steps of a three story building. The first floor was a pizzeria. When she walked inside, there were balloons, streamers, party hats, children, and silence. They were all sitting and staring at Piper standing in the doorway. The plates were greasy and empty on the dirty, table clothes.

One of the boys picked up a shard of bone off his plate and picked at his yellow teeth.

"Did I miss the cake?" Piper asked.

Don't be smart with strangers like that, Piper heard her father's imaginary voice warn.

One of the men by the counter said, "We're short on cake. Who are you, miss?"

"I'm Piper Hamel."

The other man said, "Would it be too much to assume you are here to save us, Ms. Hamel."

"Well," she offered, "If you have fuel for a standard Cessna, we might have some options."

"What's to keep us from taking your plane and leaving you here, Piper?" the second man asked.

The children were looking back and forth between the adults talking over their heads.

Piper bit her lower lip.

Negotiate from strength, her father would say.

Piper said, "Without more fuel, you'd just smash into a wall trying to takeoff and probably let the dead inside the space you

10

spent so much time walling off ... and I guess I have to ask, do any of you know how to fly?"

The two men looked at each other.

The first man said, "Don't mind Butch here, Piper. He's not really threatening you as much as he's just talking to hear his favorite noise. I'm Alan Baker."

The men behind Piper closed the door to the pizzeria. She could here the iron candleholder banging on the steps as they walked back down leaving her.

"Do you have fuel I can ... could use?" Piper asked, "Or do you know where there is any?"

Butch scratched at his scraggly face.

He said, "We can take you to the roof. You can look north by northwest over the wall. Just inside the edge of the 'dead sea' out there you will see a large, white tank in a busted paddock. We were discussing at one point taking some shots at it and seeing if we could blow a hole through the pests and maybe make a run for a new place."

Piper asked, "Why didn't you?"

The children looked back at her as she spoke. One girl slid off her party hat and held it in her lap over her nice dress.

Baker answered, "It's a stupid idea for one. We go somewhere else and they follow us. We get there and there are more waiting. We might need the bullets either for when they get in or when we decide to opt out. And besides, making loud noises is what brought them here in the first place."

Piper said, "If we can get the fuel, I can fly everyone out a few at a time."

"To where?" the boy picking his teeth with the bone asked.

"Liam," Butch snapped. "Mind your business."

Baker asked, "To where?"

Piper shrugged. "Do you know of a safe place to land close by?"

The girl that took off her party hat answered, "The Moon?"

11

Butch said, "Gail, just … okay, just celebrate Marty's birthday, kids."

The kids all looked down and stayed quiet. Liam started carving in the table with the bone.

"No place comes to mind, Piper," Baker explained. "Also, there is no way to get to the fuel. You may have just moved in to your last address."

"And you weren't invited," Butch added.

"Party crasher," Liam said.

"Liam!" Butch yelled.

"Party pooper," Gail said.

All the kids giggled. Piper counted nine of them.

"Gail, come on now!" Butch huffed.

Make yourself useful, Piper, her dad would yell.

She said, "If there is nowhere to go, we need to get the infected to leave."

"What's an infected?" Gail asked.

"The pests," Liam answered.

Butch dropped his head. "She has a point, Alan. We've never just asked them to go."

Piper said, "If I can lead the pests away and keep them away, would that be worth hauling in the fuel for me and letting me have a tank full?"

The men looked at each other and back at Piper.

"Yes," they said in unison.

Piper said, "I'll need a few things to set up, but I can do it."

"Is this a 'stone soup' trick where we end up giving you all our supplies and you suddenly fly away in your miraculously fueled plane?" Baker asked.

"No," Piper said, "I just need some stuff you probably have in your trash around this triangle."

Baker said, "Well, go nuts, Piper, and free Haven from the plague of pests that surrounds us."

Piper turned to head for the door. She looked over her shoulder at the kids gathered in a circle watching her leave.

12

She said, "Happy Birthday, Marty."

The kids all looked at each other with eyes wide. Piper looked away and opened the door to the pizzeria.

Liam said, "Marty's dead."

"Liam!"

****

Piper played her many sounds.
She did flee across the ground.
The pests followed her through the land.
She took them all as if by the hand.
The bargain was kept on her end,
But the Baker and Butch here tried to resend.
That was not cool, you see.
So the lives of the children became her fee.

****

Piper stood on the ladder looking over the wall with her binoculars. She signaled the far corner. After a couple seconds, the popping and crackling started. As she expected, all the heads snapped in that direction. After a few moments, she signaled them to start again. They played the pattern as she had showed them.

The crowd began to shift in that direction.

She signaled the other corner. The brick was draw across the grate and the heads below her snapped back the other way. As the dead wavered, she signaled both sides.

After a few moments, they began to part slightly creating a break in their ranks.

Piper put her feet on the outside of the ladder and slid down to the ground without touching the rungs.

"How do we know you'll come back?" Baker asked as he helped her shoulder her heavy pack.

"A deal is a deal," Piper explained.

She took two deep breaths and then burst out of the gate.

The dead on both sides of the gap turned back. The crowd slowly closed back on her as she ran through the gauntlet. Her pack clanked and caused them to hone in on her more easily.

The outer edge was too far, but she had to get outside their lines if this was all going to work.

All things worth doing are a challenge, Piper's dad would say.

She pressed on as they reached out for her. By the time she began to clear the back of the crowd, their fingers grazed over her shirt and the material of her pack.

She stumbled free of them, but they pursued her still.

She couldn't just run away from them. She had to make the full circle like she planned. Piper tried to control her breathing as she put distance between herself and Haven. She paced out through broken cars and discarded bones.

Piper circled around in an arc as she banked around the edge of the mob. They lined up behind her. She took out a pan and hammer she had fashioned together. They made a crisp crack each time she released the pan into the hammer. The dead began to turn away from the walls and follow after her as she continued to circle. She tried not to go too fast to lose any of them, but she jogged along to stay out of their hands.

When she got back to the side with the gate again, the crowd packed behind her and pushed to catch up to her position.

She switched her pan and hammer for a pipe and megaphone. Piper brought the threaded end up to her mouth and honked out a sour note that made the corpses growl more.

They followed her over the slope away from Haven as the townspeople watched in amazement.

****

Piper had to crawl carefully through the ditch to keep from getting spotted. As they continued to pursue her last trajectory, she sidled along behind the rearguard.

She took to her feet again once she saw the stragglers vanish over the hill.

One of them grabbed her wrist as she walked by an overturned delivery truck. She started to scream, but clapped her other hand over her mouth. She pulled away from his grasp silently. The pain stung her wrist and she looked down in horror at the long scratch across her skin.

That's all it took.

"It's me, Piper," Liam said as he stepped out of his hiding place.

She whispered, "What are you doing here?"

"I came to warn you," he said. "They will kill you, if you go back."

"Then, I'll just leave," Piper said.

"You have to help us," he begged.

Piper knelt down, "I did help you, Liam."

"No," Liam said, "You have to fly the other children out of Haven."

"What about your families?" Piper asked, "And how could I get the plane fueled?"

Liam whispered, "They ate our families. If we stay, they'll give each of us a 'birthday party' until none of us are left."

Piper just stared.

Liam added, "Some of them went to find more food. We can try it while most of them are gone."

Piper said, "They left too soon. They'll lead them back in. I made that same mistake once, too."

"Please help them," Liam begged.

"We'll need a plan," Piper said.

****

Baker and Butch ran from the plane to the side of the compound where they heard the moans echoing.

Piper slipped in and began fueling the plane.

She heard them walking up behind her. She nearly spilled as she whirled around.

Piper said, "Get inside quick."

Gail led the other seven children into the rainbow painted door.

"Where is Liam?" Piper grunted as she walked the plane around to face down the avenue.

Gail said, "He said to just go."

Piper brought the engine back to life, "We can't do that."

The moans picked up from the other direction. Baker and Butch ran back across the avenue without looking at the plane.

"How is he doing that?" Piper asked.

Then, she saw the first of the dead step out on the sidewalk.

"How did they get in?" Gail asked.

Piper answered, "The others led them back. Where's Liam?"

Gail pointed up to the rooftops.

Piper leaned out of the plane and waved for Liam to come down. He shook his head as he set down the noise maker he had been using to create the first set of fake moans. He pulled up his sleeve and showed the bite mark around his forearm.

Piper frowned and nodded. She got back inside as she began to roll the Cessna forward.

The heads of the monsters trying to walk into their path exploded as they were picked off from the rooftop. The avenue filled at the end with the dead. Piper pulled up earlier than she should. The plane shuddered as she treated it like a hotrod.

She kept it level as her wheels pulled up over the reaching hands of the dead.

****

Liam sacrificed his life
To save us from the knife
So Piper could fly us on to peace
To a safe landing and relief.

This is why we must know
what they did to save us so
we never forget their sacrifice
that brought us all to paradise.
Sadly, but as Piper's plan was hatched,
Liam was bitten before she got scratched.
She would land before she turned.
From her the art of sound we learned.
To this day she circles around
Using sound to protect our town.
This is the reason we all recite
this loving tribute every night.

****

Piper leveled the plane and continued toward the sun with all the children inside.

Gail said, "Liam is going to be eaten since he stayed back in the town."

Piper kept her eyes forward and her voice low. "He may be the one doing the eating, Gail."

"What are we going to do, Piper?"

"Hope for the light to guide us to a safe place somewhere."

Gail and Piper listened to the steady sound of the engines as they flew above the world.

About the Author

Jay Wilburn

Jay Wilburn was a public school teacher for 16 years. He left to care for his younger son and to be a full-time writer in beautiful Conway, South Carolina where he lives with his wife and two sons.

He was featured in *Best Horror of the Year vol. 5* with editor Ellen Datlow. He has published many horror and speculative fiction stories. His first novel, *Loose Ends: A Zombie Novel*, is available now. *Time Eaters* will be released by Perpetual Motion Machine Publishing. He was a featured author with Hazardous Press at the 2013 World Horror Convention. He was included in the limited edition *Best of Dark Moon of Digest*. His short story, "Bully," appeared in Source Point Press' super-hero anthology, Alter Egos Volume II.

He is a columnist for Dark Eclipse and for Revolt Daily. Follow his many dark thoughts at JayWilburn.com and @AmongTheZombies on Twitter.

Skipping School

by John Hunt

Scriiiiitch. Scraaaatch.

They were coming for Jonah. Over the past few hours the shuffling and scratching drew closer. If he remained quiet, their digging became less urgent, like they were lost or forgot what they were doing. Fear squeezed a whimper from his chest and the digging intensified; scriiiitch, scraaaatch, scriiitch-scraaatch, scriitch-scraatch, scritch-scratch, scritch-scratch. Jonah held his breath, his lips a tight white line, only a suggestion of a mouth. The scratching sounds became feeble, as though they were losing interest.

Jonah knew what made those noises, could picture them seeking him, squirming and clawing through the rubble for him, always hungry.

****

Jonah's day started out simple enough. Skip school with his girlfriend, hang out at his house, get high, maybe make out a little and hope for some third base action. He and Ashley smoked a joint, enjoying the lethargic high while watching *The Hangover* on DVD. Jonah was sliding his hand up Ashley's Catholic school skirt while knowing she noticed, but pretending in that cool way of hers that she didn't. She draped her arms over the back of the couch, a signal for him to continue, while acting as though she was watching the movie, oblivious to his advancing hand. Her skin's warmth, the excitement of what *might* happen, threatened to chase away his high. He inched his hand upwards, delighting in her smooth skin and getting a quick glimpse of her white underpants with a pink heart positioned right over the *spot*. His heart almost burst from the vision. He wanted to freeze the moment, prolong the excitement a simple pair of underpants elicited from him. Screams, so high and pain-filled, destroyed the intimacy as completely as a knock on the head with a hammer. He peered out the window, eyebrows drawn down. He recoiled, his hand clinching the meat of

Ashley's thigh. She squealed, but he'd forgotten about her. He was watching the impossible occur on his front lawn.

Standing on the grass was a woman, a postal worker, held firm by two men with blood all over them. One man had his mouth around her bicep and his jawed worried at the meat. Blood fell, a red waterfall, from her arm to splash on the grass. Her cries dripped terror and pain. Leaning in, the other man opened his mouth to latch teeth onto her shoulder, but she snapped his head back with a thrust of her palm and his teeth clacked together on empty air. The postal worker fell, tripped by another lady in an awful mustard yellow top and hair-net lying on the lawn. The mustard lady pulled herself up, digging and chewing her way into the postal worker's stomach. The screams reached a higher pitch.

What the hell was in that bud he smoked? He'd heard sometimes the stuff was laced with LSD causing you to see some weird shit, this couldn't be real, could it? He needed to know if Ashley saw the same thing because two people wouldn't have the same delusion would they? "Is some postal worker getting eaten on my front lawn right now, or am I just high as shit?"

"Jonah, you idiot, this is real! Look at the lunch lady. Where is the rest of her body? How is she moving like that? And look at the farmer in the red hat. His head is barely attached to his neck. It looks like half his head has been eaten. How is he still moving?"

Jonah looked, frowned, wondering how he missed that. Was that *his* lunch lady? She was shorn in half above the waist and her intestines trailed behind her, red and slimy, a sharp contrast to the green lawn. The postal worker stopped screaming. Her eyes staying open, staring at the sky and twitching and jerking as they tore into her, feeding. Jonah puked on the window. It splashed back onto him and Ashley.

"Jesus Jonah!"

He wiped his mouth with the back of his hand, "We gotta call the police. This is crazy! Dead things on my front lawn eating people. Where are the goddamn cops? Go ten miles over the speed limit and a hundred of them fall out of the sky, but have a group of *things* eating a civil servant in front of your house and none are around? My parents pay their salaries!"

"I'll call them," Ashley said.

Gunshots sounded in an off beat staccato. They flinched with each one.

"It's busy! 911 is busy!"

"I'm gonna get my Dad's gun."

He stood and Ashley pulled on his arm, keeping him there and said, "Look, there's a cop now."

"A Christmas miracle in May. Hallelujah!"

The police car, lights flashing, sirens keening, crested the hill and for a brief second, Jonah felt some respect for police officers because they put themselves in danger for the sake of others. The feeling abated when the police car sideswiped a parked car and careened away with a foot to spare from a house near the base of the hill. Jonah squinted to see who was behind the wheel. The police car, out of control, swerved toward his house. It wasn't slowing down.

"*Move-outta-the-way!*" He dove to the side as the cruiser smashed through the bay window. The cruiser's grille entered Jonah's living room striking Ashley in the chest and carrying her away, through the back wall, as though she was never there. Glass flew, invisible razors exploding outwards embedding themselves everywhere. Continuing through, with Ashley pinned to the hood, the car tore through drywall, furniture and wood, destroying everything before it. A love seat spun through the air and landed on Jonah, smashing into his calf, and he yelped. The back of the chair covered him entirely. Only his injured leg stuck out and the image of the Wicked Witch in the *The Wizard of Oz*, her striped feet pinned under the house, flashed through his mind. Dust settled, thick, stinging Jonah's eyes and coating his throat. He peeked through his arms cocooning his head and hissed from the throbbing in his calf. He didn't think it was broken, but it sure hurt. A lot. Can you even break a calf? A loud crack ripped through the house. Jonah pushed at the love seat, cringing at the sharp pain in his leg, listening to the sound of the cruiser's engine a short distance away when the ceiling crashed down on top of him.

It was thunder in his ears, a rolling noise, endless, and Jonah screamed, squeezing his eyes closed so tight he thought his eyebrows were probably touching his cheeks. More weight settled on the love seat crushing his leg beneath it. Would this stupid love-seat hold up under the weight of the second floor? What a sucky day! Jonah, like a turtle in a shell, was too afraid to poke his head out or even open his eyes. It seemed forever, like an entire history class, before the noise of the settling debris stopped. Only ticks and light cracks could be heard intermittently. Jonah whispered, "Fuck my life!"

He flicked his lighter on and the light was an orange glow moving with the falling flakes of dust. After a quick glimpse he flicked it off. The love seat falling on him had protected him from the upper floor's collapse. Encapsulated in a little protective cave of ugly eighties furniture, Jonah tried to find relief for his throbbing leg, but it was pinned immobile. The image of Ashley being struck by the police cruiser's hungry grille left no doubt in his mind she had been killed. His heart ached and his stomach roiled, but he had to force those feelings away and try to figure out a way out.

He pushed on the love seat to free himself. It didn't budge. He put his hands on the ground and tried to use his body to push it up and away, but all he managed to do was cause the pain in his leg to flare up. Heavy breathing inhaled the thick dust and he was wracked with coughs. When he stopped he heard… nothing. The police cruiser, sirens and engine, were silent. Jonah jumped by a man's surprised yelp. The scream became a plea as a man said, "No, no, no. Get away you little bitch! Don't do that! Please! Ah-ah! Nooooo! That hurts!"

The terror-filled screams were muffled but Jonah's body shook in empathetic horror. Ripping, chewing and slurping came from the direction of the shrieks and Jonah knew there must be one of those things in here eating the poor cop in the cruiser. The cries turned to whimpers, half hearted exhausted pleas, before the sound stopped altogether.

Trapped with a monster in his living room, Jonah sobbed until exhaustion forced sleep upon him.

He awoke, in reluctant lengthy stages, to the ringing of his cell phone. An insistent, bothersome noise rousing him from lethargy.

The short movement for his cell phone erupted pain all over his body. He fumbled his cell phone out and answered it without even glancing at the name.

"Hello?"

"Jonah! Thank God you answered!"

"Mom?"

"Yes honey, where are you?"

"Is Dad with you?"

"Yes, he's right here beside me. Now, where are you?"

"Mom," he started to cry, hearing her voice, he couldn't help it and said, "Monsters, *hic*, ate our mailman, uh woman."

"Yes honey, and that must have been terrible, but where the hell are *you*?"

Still crying, he calmed himself enough to answer, "At home. The roof collapsed on me. Some cop car rammed into our house, and it ran into Ashley." His tears overtook him and he blubbered out, "I think she's dead."

"Jonah? Can you get out of there?"

"No. I'm trapped. Dad's stupid chair pinned my leg. I can't even feel it anymore. The roof is sitting on top of it and I can't move it off."

He heard his mom bark at his dad, "I told you to get rid of that stupid, and very ugly, chair!"

His dad, distant in the background said, "Like you knew something like this would happen. You've always hated that chair!"

His mother sighed into the phone and said, "Do you have anything to dig yourself out with?"

"No, all I got is a lighter, cell phone and some small, but good bud."

"Drugs! You have drugs? Where did you get it? What have you been up to?"

"Mom!" Jonah interrupted, "Are you seriously gonna lecture me now? At this moment?"

"You're right, sorry, but we will have a talk about this later. We're coming for you, but it may be a while alright, Jonah? Jonah?"

"Quiet for a sec mom, I think I hear something."

Scritch-scratch, scritch-scratch.

"Mom, I think something is in here with me," he whispered.

A moan issued from the darkness, high-pitched and feminine, and Jonah had an idea of who made it.

"Mom, hurry. It's Ashley. She's coming for me. Please hurry!"

The scratching became faster, desperate, hungry.

"We're coming. Hang in there. We're coming as fast as we can!"

He hung up and looked around using the light from his cell phone as a flashlight. He pointed it in the direction of the digging but could barely see from under the chair pressing into him. The digging slowed and he relaxed his strained muscles when, for some reason, the way he turned caused explosive pain to radiate from his leg where it had been pinned by the chair. He screeched out a cry and forced himself to stop when a new moan sounded and digging escalated with a fury. He was confused until he remembered the police officer was Ashley's virgin meal. Coldness pulsed through his twisted frame as he realized two creatures hungered for him now. And they were digging through the rubble to get him.

He kept as quiet as he could and soon enough, the mining for him slowed and the moans quieted. He exhaled and cursed when his cell phone rang again, triggering moans and frantic scratching. '*Are you freaking kidding me?*' thought Jonah, '*Dead things start taking over the town and I'm suddenly popular.*'

Still, he answered it. Teenage programming compelled him to. "What!?"

"Hey Jonah? What's up man?"

It was Jake, an acquaintance from school.

"Other than dead people eating live people? Oh, not too much, moron!" Jonah whispered.

The scratching and digging increased in tempo.

"Yeah, I know, pretty crazy right?"

"What do you want?"

"You uh, got any bud?"

"What!?"

"Bud man! Weed!"

"Are you nuts?"

"Look man, I haven't heard from my parents or my little sister. She's six years old, man."

Silence from Jonah. He was imagining what happened to them. A shiver chattered his teeth.

"I just need to chill you know? I want to feel good about something and stop feeling so freaking scared you know?"

"I got a little bud on me but there is more around the house. My private stashes, but I'm trapped here. I've got a chair crushing my leg and the roof sitting on top of me. You can have some, but you gotta get me outta here."

"For real? Your house fell on you? Epic! I gotta see this."

Jonah heard the fumbling of a phone against fabric and some breathing and then, "Holy hairy goat sack! There are like five of them chilling on your front lawn. And your house! It's destroyed! You're in that mess?"

Jake lived across the street. They used to be close friends, but high school had a way of distancing people.

"Yeah, I told you I'm trapped in here and I can't move. And Ashley is in here with me. She's coming for me."

"Dude. That sucks."

"Can you help me? She's getting *closer*. She's freaking moaning at me."

"I don't know man. I don't want to get eaten. That's probably my number one way of how not to die."

"You got your Dad's rifle right? Just shoot them from your house all safe like and then come over and dig me out."

"How do you kill something that's dead?"

"Shoot them in the head, I guess. You gotta help me. I can't even feel my leg anymore and I'm cramping up all over."

He couldn't either. His leg felt separate from his body, an emptiness below his knee. His hip hurt from the way he curled on his side and his back and neck throbbed from lack of movement.

"Ah, man!" Jake complained.

"Just try!"

"Alright, but you owe me man. Big time. One monster blunt, as big as my forearm."

"You get me outta here and you can have my whole stash."

"Okay. Hopefully, I'll see you soon."

Jake hung up and Jonah winced as he tried to stretch himself out in the cramped space. The digging sounds had stopped. He didn't know whether that boded well or not. He hoped Ashley and the cop had just forgotten about him. He was about to fall into an exhausted sleep when the sharp report of a rifle startled him to alertness. His phone rang again and he answered, "Yeah?'

"One shot, one kill! This rifle is sick! It has a scope and everything! The head shot worked! Dropped as fast as an Italian soccer player in the World Cup!"

"Good man, just please hurry up, my leg man, it's f'd up."

"Alright, I'm coming man."

He hung up and while the rifle's report echoed, Jonah wondered how long his leg could last without any fresh blood supply. From his first aid course he had learned about tourniquets. It constricted the area above a bleeding wound so that the blood wouldn't flow before coagulation. Jonah had learned from the course that a tourniquet must be loosened every ten minutes otherwise adjacent flesh would die from lack of oxygenated blood. He had been stuck here for awhile now, a few hours at least, and the chair pinning his leg to the floor was acting the same way as a tourniquet would, yet he hadn't been able to relieve any of the pressure. Could his leg be dead already? He couldn't tell. He couldn't feel his leg at all and that scared him. He once again fell into an exhausted sleep.

****

Sunlight and dust filtered down onto his face. Inhaling the dust Jonah coughed rubbing his dry throat raw.

"There he is! I can hear him."

"Jonah!" said his mom.

His lungs burned and his throat scraped raw, but he couldn't stop coughing. His mother's eyes peered at him from over the love seat.

"Jonah! Thank God!" She thrust a water bottle at him and his palsied hand grasped it. His arm flinched back as his cramped muscles protested and the open bottle fell to the carpet and rolled under his hip. Still coughing he reached for it, fingers probing and brought it to his mouth and drank greedily.

"Hurry! Let's get him out!"

The excavating made more dust and debris filter down and Jonah covered his mouth and nose to prevent another coughing fit. Freed from the chair, his accidental cave, he was confused when his mother screamed and fainted. His Dad and Jake stared down his body in open mouthed horror.

Jonah followed their eyes. "*Nooooooooo!*" he said, "*Ashley! C'mon!*"

Ashley was chewing on his calf and, in some spots, was down to his shin bone. Chunks of flesh were pushing out her cheeks. The chair tourniquet now released, the blood flowed into his leg and and splashed from his wounds onto Ashley's contented face. The cop was feasting on his foot. The flesh was torn away in ragged strips, his heel all but gone. Jonah jumped when Ashley's head exploded from a rifle round. The loud report throbbing in his ears. Jake had shot her. And then he shot the cop as well.

"I'm sorry Jonah," his father said. His dad's eyes shiny pools as he gave Jake a nod, a pat on the shoulder and walked away.

"Sorry? For what? Get me out of here! I need help."

"We can't Jonah," Jake said.

"What do you mean you can't? I'm bleeding out here!"

"Your parents told me. They were listening to the Emergency Broadcast System. They were told that people become those things in two ways. Dying or being bit. It looks like you've been hit by both barrels," Jake said. He raised the rifle and pointed it at Jonah's head. "The only way they don't come back is if the brain is destroyed."

"WTF dude! Jake! C'mon! I'll be fine! Just get me some help, a bandage or something! I'll recover and we'll smoke a huge bong and talk about how close I came to dying!"

"Sorry man. Its gotta be done." Jake said. He lowered his gun, eyes flitting over to Jonah's dad's shaking back and whispered, "Would you mind telling me where your stash is? Don't want to waste it right?" He winked at Jonah, actually freaking winked at him.

Jonah was getting ready to tell Jake to eat a steaming pile, tell him to get lost, but reconsidered and sighed, "In the basement meat freezer, under the chicken in an empty ice cream container."

"Thanks man."

"Whatever."

Jake shot him in the head thinking of how he'd smoke a huge bong in Jonah's memory. As soon as he figured out how to get the stash without Jonah's parents knowing.

About the Author

John Hunt

A busy father of four, John Hunt is a published author who started writing in late 2009. Most of his writing is done during his spare time.

He lives and works in the city of Guelph, Ontario, Canada with his wife, four children, a dog and two cats.

Skinwalker

by Niccolo Skill

If it could speak, I know what it would say. "Come here," it would snarl through animal teeth. "Come, let us chat, let us get acquainted; get to know each other. Something to eat perhaps?" And it would laugh. But it wouldn't be a human laugh, not the kind full of humor or love or caring; it would be something less, like the growl of a beast only half-alive. "Why do you look so afraid? I don't bite, not like them." It would nod its head toward one of the Carrion, and smile with its cannibal teeth.

The Carrion would look in through the windows, between the boards and the shattered glass. They would reach in, groping mindlessly with their broken and bloodied fingers like horny adolescents. Snarls would seep like oil from their teeth, what few remained. Jaws snapping and gangly limbs twisting, they would force their way through the barriers as if opening a clam shell, ready to savor the meat inside. Their stench would precede them, wafting through the hollow halls even without a carrying breeze. They would shamble, stumble, limp, and crawl. Whatever it took, they would do it, even if it meant losing more of themselves. They would shed an arm just to fit through the narrow windows, just to eat. Just to survive.

It would lead them, like an officer in the thick of the battle. The Carrion horde would follow; puppets carried by their marionette strings. They would march on to their prize, to me, led by their unholy patriarch. And it would smile, and it would say, "They bite, yes, but I am so much worse, so much more." But it couldn't talk, couldn't even smile. Its teeth were hidden by unmoving lips. It didn't move or speak like a human, it merely looked like one. It was untouched by time or rot, not like the Carrion that had decomposed to little more than skeletons. They were grazing cadavers, roving corpses. But it was so much more. It moved with a liquid grace, walking on the balls of its feet and strutting like a big cat ready to pounce. Its gaze was predatory, its face emotionless. Its silver hair flowed behind it like a mane, its fingers arched into claws, its head weaved like an entranced cobra. The Skinwalker, backed by its reanimated legion, advanced on us. Next to me, Mark swore and Gabby echoed him.

It chased us upstairs, cornering us in the master bedroom that we all shared on uncertain nights. Mark slammed the door and I toppled the bookshelf in front of it, just before it absorbed the full weight of a Carrion. By then, Gabby had already loaded the revolver and snapped the cylinders back into place with a flick of her wrist. We all carried weapons, but the majority of our firepower was downstairs, in the backroom. It'd been months since the last attack, weeks since we last saw even a single Carrion, and we somehow got the idea that we were safe.

Then, the Skinwalker wandered into town, walking down Main Street like it belonged. He— no, it— was the first Skinwalker Gabby and Mark had ever seen, and only my second. They started popping up after the initial outbreak, when the infection was first discovered. While most people were devolved into Carrion, things that were less than human, others were made into something more. Some people said it was steroids; that copious amounts of the juice induced the Skinwalker mutation. Others proposed that the uncontrolled cell growth of cancer was magnified by the virus, resulting in the Skinwalker's internal... peculiarities. Me? I think they're demons.

Mark slid his crowbar off his belt and into the eye socket of an ambitious Carrion. Immediately it was replaced by another, which promptly caught a .357 round. They were endless, coming just as quickly as we could bring them down. Carrion after Carrion dropped in the doorway, which was slowly being pried open by the growing pile of bodies. Underneath the metallic clang of the crowbar and the crack of the revolver, was the unmistakable growl of the advancing Skinwalker.

Splinters were flung off the door as the unrelenting dead muscled their way in. Pounding fists and gouging fingers tore the aged wood to pieces. Shoulders and rotting foreheads repeatedly slammed against the frame, while corroding teeth vainly gnawed at the hinges.

"Mark, help me here!" I yelled over the battering sound of the assault. We braced our shoulders against the door, rocking back and forth with the undulating power of the Carrion. I glanced back in time to see Gabby reloading her pistol, curiously hesitating for a moment. When she looked up and caught my stare, she tilted the gun forward, showing me the half-empty six-cylinder. We'd always discussed this, the three of us. Would we let each other die by the horde, or we would take the easy way, the quick way? Would any of us be able to endure the pain to save our friends a bullet? Would we be able to watch, as someone else endured, too selfish to waste a shot?

The door shattered, throwing Mark and I to Gabby's feet. The Skinwalker stood in the doorway, all silver mane and predatory physique, a mound of twice-dead at its feet. Two long strides brought it to our feet; one more landed its foot on Mark's abdomen. All the air left his lungs at once, rushing out in an audible whoosh. My arm naturally intertwined with Gabby's and we wriggled ourselves out from underneath Mark, just before the Skinwalker hoisted him up by his throat.

There was no definition of muscle in its arm, no signs of strain or effort. Its expression didn't change, holding fast in its emotionless state. Even with Mark struggling, kicking and swiping with his crowbar, the Skinwalker didn't flinch or waver in the slightest.

The first time I ever saw a Skinwalker, it was holding my brother by his neck, more than a foot off the floor. It had the same white hair, pale skin, and white pupils as the one that had Mark in its grasp. It was like there was no color in it at all, just black and white, even its clothes. My brother was going blue, couldn't breathe under the thing's iron grip, but still had the fight in him to claw out one of his attacker's eyes. The eye popped out, and his fingernails scraped away a patch of skin. There wasn't any bone beneath it though, not even the pink-red flesh of a man, but something altogether different. Then it sank its claws into my brother's heart, and I sprinted away, to the garage. I revved up the Chevy and peeled out of our driveway. Standing in the frame of our front door was the Skinwalker, its long gray hair waving behind it like a dying snake. Where its fingers should have been were long bone claws, tapered like ice picks. Its face was half-human, the other half was something less. Something more.

As Gabby leveled her gun, hammer already cocked, the monster in front of us pierced Mark's skull. This one had the same ice pick fingers, the ivory shining under the artificial light. They were on every finger, on both hands, like the retractable claws of a big cat.

The Carrion had swarmed the door; a few were already biting away chunks of Mark's corpse. Their teeth clamped down on his flesh, not puncturing at first, but pressing down hard enough to make me grimace. When they did pierce, blood sprouted like young flowers, squirting out of a torn artery. Jagged teeth left crooked and misshapen holes in his arms, his legs, his face. Some bites were shallow, peeling away strips of skin and minimal muscle; others tore down to the bone.

I smashed a window, clearing the broken glass with the blade of my knife. Gabby went out before me, sliding out feet-first, gun held firmly in her left hand. She snapped off a shot just before she dropped out of view. I watched the Skinwalker's right shoulder recoil from the slug. It stared me down when I slid down to the ground.

Gabby and I landed lightly, considering our second story drop. I noticed she was crying, even though she was wiping them away as they came. We could still hear the Carrion moving inside the house: walking unevenly, dragging themselves across the wooden floors, chewing on the bodies of either Mark or their fallen comrades.

"My God," Gabby sighed, leaning her back against the side of the house, still wiping away teardrops.

"Gabby, we need to keep moving," I panted. My heart was racing and I couldn't breathe properly. Rest sounded delicious, but nothing we could revel in quite yet.

"I'm so tired," she wheezed. "Just a minute, they're too busy with… " She let the sentence trail off; we both knew what she meant. "The Skinwalker won't be down here until we're long gone, we can rest just for a bit."

"Gabby, Skinwalkers don't-" but I didn't get a chance to finish, not before the siding of the house burst. An ivory-tipped hand caught Gabby's ponytail and pulled her flat against the wall. She was screaming, but I didn't know if it was from fear or pain. I prayed for fear. I grabbed her hand and pulled her to me, just enough to stretch her hair. A swift downward stroke of my knife freed her, but I groaned when I saw her blonde hair dyed strawberry.

Her hand went to the back of her head, and came away bloody. "No," she whimpered. "No, no, no." She looked up at me, probably for support, maybe just an 'It'll be alright', but I gave her nothing. I stared back, disbelief in my eyes that a single monster had taken both of my friends from me. I was still staring into her eyes when she put the gun into her mouth and shot herself.

She slumped to the ground, and I could swear I saw a pale eye glaring at me through the puncture in the building. If the hole had been big enough, I imagine there would have been a cold grin below that pale iris.

The ground was wet from morning dew and I slid more than once as my feet pounded against the sodden earth. My shoes were soaked with the moisture and my jeans clung to my ankles, numbing my feet and hurting my progress. It wasn't long until I fell.

Carrion banged on the window to my left hard enough to crack it. Hair-sized veins spider webbed out from the main fractures and gave way under the accumulated weight of the horde. Groping hands reached for me, squeezing at nothing and swiping at everything. Scrambling to my feet, I sprinted to the front lawn, sprinted to the Chevy.

As I rounded the corner, my momentum left me all at once. It took me a while to realize there were claw-tipped fingers holding me in place. It lifted me by my throat, forcing my entire weight down on my neck. I heard my spine pop. The Skinwalker looked up at me with those dead eyes, staring straight into my blue ones. "I won," it would say if it could speak. "I killed your friends, and I'm going to kill you. Oh, why so glum? At least the Carrion won't get to you." And it would smile, and chuckle that death rattle laugh.

They never eat, never drink or sleep or even rest. Even the Carrion eat, even if their diet consists of still-living people. But never the Skinwalkers, I've never even seen them bite to infect, if that's even possible. Would you rise up as one of them, possessed by whatever evil drove them, or would you devolve into a Carrion? Who knows.

My skin started to split under the bone nails. Pinpricks of blood welled up and stained its ice pick claws. The scarlet pikes bit deeper into my neck. I could feel them caressing my arteries, rubbing against my windpipe and silently threatening me with death. I flailed, just as my brother and Mark had, kicking hard against its chest and abdomen, occasionally landing a shot in its groin. I slashed with my knife, back and forth across its wrist in a vain attempt to sever its hand. I turned my knife to its face, slashing down and across, peeling away a sheet of skin in the process. I wish I hadn't.

It wasn't bone, or exposed muscle. It was something entirely different. It wasn't as smooth as bone, or as hard; and it was black, a pitch black that allowed no deviation in color. There was no nuance shade of gray or even a slight reflection of light. It was a black abyss that composed the Skinwalker's body, shaped into the form of a man. A slight ripple shook the colorless mass, ending at the edges of torn human skin. The Carrion were undead, rotting, still-walking corpses, but they were at least human once. The thing before me looked human on the outside, but beneath that fragile layer of skin was something inhuman, something that never was. It was otherworldly, a thing that had no place in this mortal plane.

Was that it? After all the speculation, was that the answer? Was that outer wrapping of skin the only thing keeping those monsters grounded in this reality? The Skinwalkers weren't zombies, not the products of a virus, but something unfathomable to the human mind.

Were they demons? Demons that had broken free from hell, casting forth their pestilence and following in its wake. The Devil himself may have been wandering the earth. Maybe he'd been imprisoned, detained in the violent coup of his underlings while they devoured the world.

I was amazed how my mind kept working, even after those cannibal teeth tore out my throat.

****

My hair is silver, as pale as my skin and undoubtedly my eyes. There are ivory claws where fingers used to be. They click together when I try to clench a fist. My steps aren't heel-to-toe anymore, I stalk along on the balls of my feet as if ready to spring. My skin doesn't feel quite right, like there isn't enough of it. Maybe I'll peel it off one day.

I walk down Main Street as if I belong, as if I have a place in this world.

About the Author

Niccolo Skill

Niccolo Skill is a horror author currently residing in his home state of New York. His work has appeared or is forthcoming in PseudoPod, Fifty Word Stories, and Another 100 Horrors.

The Invention

by Joshua Werner

Who would have thought that the two most significant events to affect human history would happen so close together in time? One event so horrible and catastrophic that it expedited years of research and ingenuity to create the other. Perhaps it's always been this way. Perhaps the world needs gruesome violence beyond its comprehension to be awoken, to be inspired.

The Human Holocaust took place in December of 2015. Only 14 months have passed, but the days before the Holocaust feel so long ago I sometimes forget what they were like. I remember them being glorious of course, but my memories of that time contrast my day-to-day life so greatly that they seem hard to believe, too good to be true. I frequently second guess myself, my very life. As if maybe it never happened, maybe my memories are simply an elaborate dream I had, and that the world has always been this horrible. Luckily, for my own sanity, human beings have the innate desire to record their own history, a reminder that my memories are intact. And those records will litter this planet with meaninglessness centuries after our extinction. I can't help but wonder... everything that every nation fought for, worked toward, strived for... what the hell was the point of it?

Richard says it was God. Or Jesus Christ. Or maybe a God/Jesus tag team match where they took turns holding the magnifying glass. Watching us run about, trying to stay on our paths to do our jobs, to build our structures, to bring food to our families, all the while avoiding the intensified beam of sunlight that was striking us all down. All the while pretending that the sun had gone down a little early, and that the darkness surrounding us had nothing to do with the shadow being cast by Jesus' size 13 boot smashing our homes and spilling our guts.

At first he claimed it was the Rapture. But I called him out on that one. First of all, if this was the Rapture then we sure as hell went to different Sunday Schools. Secondly, the people that had been taken were supposed to be the faithful right? Well I'd sure seen my fair share of scumbags taken, and not in a manner that looked the slightest bit heavenly. Richard went on to quote other Bible passages, continuing to push the idea that the Human Holocaust was God's will. He argued plenty of reasons for what would have driven our Creator to snuff us out; most of them pretty solid ones. I have no argument against a motive. The human race probably deserves this, and worse. But my vote is still for human error. For all the same reasons that we deserve a heavenly annihilation, we are most likely to have created this Hell on earth ourselves. Out of pure stupidity. Nothing can destroy humanity faster than humans. If there is a God, a Jesus Christ savior, a Holy Ghost, and a choir of angels; then they are certainly getting the show of their lifetime. On my jaded days I imagine them eating popcorn and placing bets. On my worst days I imagine they never existed at all. On the rest of the days I imagine they are watching us and weeping with a heavy sorrow. That it is now them who are praying for our souls.

Having an IQ of 142 is not a gift. It's a burden beyond most people's comprehension. After the event, swarms of people approached me with questions and cries for help. "Dr. Roth, will you be working towards a cure? You can help figure this out, right?"

"I'm not that kind of Doctor," I replied as I pushed through the crowd.

The 'outbreak' as they were calling it, had occurred in my own town. I was at work at the time, when the news of the outbreak appeared on the television we kept on in the laboratory. "Channel 4 bringing you the latest breaking news: It appears a contagion has broke out in this local neighborhood a mere fifteen minutes ago. The police were drawn to the scene when a man, suspected of carrying a deadly virus, was seen attacking another man on this very street. The officer had to call for backup before being able to apprehend the man, whose identity is still unknown to us at this time. One of the officers involved, as well as the man seen being attacked, appear to have been infected with this unknown virus and we do not know at this time whether or not they are still alive. Ambulances are taking the infected man, the man's victim, and the police officer to the County Hospital. We'll have more on this story as it continues to unfold." I was abhorred to see that the street sign behind the reporter had the name of my own. Some coworkers, including fellow physicist and acquaintance Stanley Atwater, urged me not to go home, that it wasn't safe. But where else would I go after work? Of course I was going home, that's what I did every day and I wasn't about to allow this event to break my pattern. I did, of course, take precautions, such as putting on a surgical mask as I pulled onto my street later that day, and I also refused to take off a pair of rubber gloves for three days until I was certain that I had cleaned and disinfected every inch of my house.

Wisconsin had never seen such commotion; the news had trampled through every television station, every website, and every paper. People began to leave their homes, crowding the expressways in an attempt to run anywhere. To run nowhere. The chain reaction of people following suit grew exponentially as known cases of infected citizens popped up in all the surrounding cities. I made the difficult choice to stay put, even when the police had evacuated the city. I refused to leave my home. Where would I have gone, anyhow? Basic logic showed that nowhere would be safe. Hysteria set in when cases began to appear in Iowa, Illinois, and the upper peninsula of Michigan. You can imagine what took place from here, nationwide. Martial Law, riots, robberies, even the Whitehouse burned to the ground. Frightened people are dangerous people. As the nation tore itself asunder, the infection spread like wildfire. The terrified masses demanding that the government do something, that they save them, did nothing but stand in the way of the government attempting to do just that. In under one month American life as we know it had spun out of control. The casualties reached horrifying numbers. Every known politician was either dead or in hiding, the only news was hearsay from the random passerby, all of Wisconsin was without power, and I found myself unable to leave my home.

Stan calls them 'Hollows'. It seemed fitting enough. It begins with some form of bodily fluid contact. The most popular form of this seems to be saliva entering the bloodstream via teeth tearing through flesh. From there the person becomes violently ill. Uncontrollable vomiting, extreme fatigue, a remarkably high fever, tremors, hallucinations, sometimes even seizures. All in a matter of minutes. Irreparable brain and organ damage average about three minutes in. The infection acts like meningoencephalitis on steroids. The first part of the brain to become inflamed is the limbic system. That means the destruction of your hippocampus. The annihilation of your amygdala. Your anterior thalamic nuclei colliding with your septum so it can crush your limbic cortex. Your habenula and fornix rupturing. For the uninformed, these aren't things you'd wish on even your worst enemy. After this, the person dies. There hasn't been a single exception. This is the most aggressive virus the human race has ever seen. But that doesn't end it. The dead person's brain then becomes reactivated. This baffled the doctors more than the infection itself. I imagine even if my Doctorate were in a medical field that no amount of education could help me to explain how or why this happens. The dead person regains certain functions and motor skills. Their organs are trashed, as is most of their brain. The limbic system supports emotions, behavior, and long-term memories. Your very identity. Without it properly functioning, you are... hollow.

I'm a physicist, not a physician. But when the population of the nation started falling to the infection and I lost contact with the rest of the world... I stopped my research and did what I could to understand the infected. They'd already been wandering all throughout my neighborhood. Slowly roaming the streets, each looking about as if they were searching for a lost friend. At that time, I hadn't seen any uninfected humans for days. I was alone, but surrounded by living corpses. So I moved the contents of my cupboards down to my basement. There I had lots of space, my laboratory equipment, and luckily a bathroom. My compulsion to buy exactly ten at a time of every item that I needed to purchase turned out to be a blessing in disguise. I was well stocked on pretty much everything. But once the cell phone towers were down and the internet connections were severed, I grew anxious. When the electricity went out I knew I had to work up the courage to leave the basement. And the *house*. Once I'd made my way up the stairs to the living room I watched through the blinds and waited patiently until there were no wandering bodies in sight. I took my truck out of the garage and putted down the road, keeping my speed low so as not to create too much noise.

It was during my stealthy 'robbery' of a large hardware chain that my fear of these roaming dead people turned to extreme curiosity. My plan to obtain a generator turned into a plan to obtain a generator and a member of the infected community. There were two of them in the store. Close to one another but seemingly completely unaware of the other's existence. One of them kept staring at a barbecue grill while the other was sitting on a riding lawn mower. I was hiding behind overpriced and oversized plastic garbage cans watching them intently. The sunlight was coming in the large glass entrance of the store and I could see them very clearly. The middle-aged man was wearing a button-down shirt with one of the sleeves torn off. The shirt was so stained with blood it was difficult to guess what color it was supposed to be. It looked as though his arm and shoulder had been clawed at and gnawed on by a lion, but of course I knew they were wounds created by the Hollows. As if their uncontrollable urge to attack people wasn't strange enough, I'd learned from the news early on that once their victim dies, and is soon after resurrected, the attacker appears to lose interest in the victim and then wanders away. But upon seeing an uninfected person they attack with no hesitation. They tear at the flesh with their teeth ferociously, but not in a manner that looks as though they're necessarily trying to eat them, but more like they're trying to destroy the person as quickly and efficiently as possible. I wondered to myself if the infection was so evolved that it had its own survival instinct. If it controlled the body's brain in a way that would force the host to help spread the infection, insuring the future of the infection by spreading it to as many people as possible. I recalled my knowledge of the Cordyceps fungi, a parasite that destroys their host's tissue to replace it with its own. Some species are capable of controlling the minds of their hosts, which are usually arthropods, to convince them to travel to a place where the fungus can find good growth conditions to better spread the infection. Did this infection hold some sort of... intelligence?

As I gazed at the wounds of the middle-aged Hollow and thought to myself about parasites, I had hardly noticed that he had begun to open and close the top of the grill he had been staring at so intently. His hands started moving slowly about in the air in front of him. It was as if he was aware that at one time he knew what that object was and what to do with it, but now he could not. The motions of his right hand resembled that of a person flipping burgers over, but it was obvious that he did not know why his hand was making the motion. Suddenly I heard a verbal noise that frightened me so bad I nearly fell backward. My heart was racing as my eyes darted back and forth between the two Hollows. Despite the gasp I had let out and the slight jostling of the garbage cans as I had clutched them, neither of the dead people seemed to have heard me. I heard the sound again, a sort of wheezy groan, and I realized it was the 20-something blonde girl that was missing part of her jaw. She was sitting atop the lawn mower and moving the steering wheel slowly back and forth while continuing to make the groaning noise, which was causing fluid to fall through the open side of her face. Strings of saliva with red streaks of blood worked their way out her mouth, down the side of her wounded face, and onto her neck. I imagined a child pretending to cut the grass and making the sounds of a mower. *You've got it girl, that's pretty close to a functioning memory.* At this point I had nearly forgotten about the generator and was now trying to decide which corpse I wanted to take home with me.

Before I could make up my mind I realized I was pushing the garbage can forward on an angle so that I could better see, and the lid to the can was sliding off. I jumped forward to try to catch it, terrified it would make a noise and alert the Hollows, but in my fumbling about I actually knocked the entire garbage can over. The girl on the mower stopped bubbling and spittling out of her mouth; her eyes glancing about every which way. The man at the grill was closer to me and when my head turned toward him I saw he was already lunging in my direction. I jumped to my feet and started tripping over myself as I was moving backwards away from the man, unwilling to turn around and remove his whereabouts from my vision. He stumbled and jerked about violently, his body nearly spasming with energy. I decided to turn and run. Everything I'd witnessed of the infected through the cracks in my blinds at home showed them to be very slow moving. I hoped that held true, but as I glanced behind me I saw that not only was the man keeping pace with me (albeit in a bizarre twitching manner), but the lawnmower girl was not far behind him. They looked absolutely super-charged with a rage I had never witnessed on a person before, living or dead. I skidded to a halt when I spotted something that could be used as a weapon. I realized them chasing me out of the store would mean my death, since there were multiple Hollows stumbling about in the parking lot. There hadn't been any around when I'd arrived, but the sound of the truck must've drawn some of them to the area.

I swung the rake towards the head of the Hollow with the chewed up arm, striking him right across his temple. *Damn it.* I'd intended to stick it right into his brain, but in my haste I hadn't turned the rake the right direction, so I'd hit him with the flat side of it. It was enough to take him to the ground though, his eyes blinking and his jaw twisting about with his mouth open wide. He looked to be in agonizing pain, but he was not making much noise nor moving about much. The girl was on top of me before I knew it, knocking me to the ground, a bubbling hiss escaping through the open side of her face. She weighed considerably less than me, so I

43

was able to throw her off and get back to my feet. I tried another Babe Ruth rake attack, but I missed her cranium and ended up hooking the side of her face, the lower prongs slipping into her meaty, torn-up, oozing cheek while another prong sunk into the side of her nose. She continued to move toward me, her arms stretched out in front of her trying to grab at my shirt. I pushed the handle of the rake forward, knocking her head backward, causing the prongs to slip out of her face with sort of 'slop' sound. The second swing entered the side of her cranium and knocked her to the ground. With a stomp of my foot I was able make the prongs do a complete disappearing act. I must've done enough damage to her brain to end her un-life, because she didn't get back up. She was mowing lawns in Hell now.

The infected man on the ground appeared to be unconscious. His body was clearly full of life, and moving and twitching, but he seemed to be in a heavy daze that allowed me to pull him by the shoulders into one of the over-sized garbage cans. I put the lid on it and wrapped the entire thing up with some chains from aisle five. The garbage can had two wheels, which allowed me to cart the corpse around like he was on a handcart. "I think I'll call you Gary," I said to my new test subject, clearly happy with myself.

With some planning, serious effort, and a handful of moments that made me wish I'd brought a second pair of pants with me, I managed to get both the backyard-chef and the generator into my truck and to my home without swapping bodily fluids with any of the Hollows. I only kept Gary alive for about one day, chained up to a pole in the basement. Once I felt like I had learned what I could from observing him, and was freaking myself out with worries of him gaining superhuman strength and breaking through the chains, I decided Gary had worn out his welcome. Donned in my clear rain poncho, bright yellow rubber kitchen gloves, and a pair of skiing goggles, I jabbed him in the head with a knife duct-taped to a pole repeatedly until there was no more motion. You'd think a genius could have come up with a more interesting way to kill a diseased homicidal creature tied up in his basement, but I was tired. Even in the truest form of death, I continued to learn from Gary for about a week, when the smell had overpowered my desire for knowledge. The stench was so horrid I began to wonder if the infection could travel around on it, like a little demon on a stinky green cloud trying to fly into my nose and mouth. Regardless of the gasmask I had fashioned out of normal household items, I continued to feel unsafe, so I disposed of my test subject's body in my neighbor's yard. I felt justified since the tree on their yard had been dropping its damn leaves all over mine for years.

I learned that the infection was overriding the nervous system in various ways. I found that fibers in the thoracic spinal cord were sending extreme jolts to the adrenal medulla every time Gary and his buddies laid eyes on the living. Despite the fact that the infected person had actually died, the infection was sparking up the nervous system and certain parts of the brain. The chromaffin cells in the medulla continued to work just fine, and the signals coming in were causing them to secrete epinephrine in large doses. In a normal person a dose half the size would cause that 'fight-or-flight' response when faced with danger. In the Hollows, this mega dose was causing an incalculable rage. It was in learning this that I fully realized the hopelessness of the world's situation. This infection had a goal: the survival of the infection. And the best way for an infection to survive was to multiply. *A parasite utilizing its host to do nothing but find and infect other hosts. Permanently destroying the parts of the brain that gave their host any identity or free will, wrecking the frontal lobe to light a fire under the amygdala, utilizing and enhancing what it needs to turn its host into a weapon.*

I knew it would be completely impossible to 'cure' any of the infected, and with the human reaction to gather with other humans when they feel frightened or threatened, they were making it that much easier for the infection to spread in a violent, swift manner. The population of the human race would plummet as the population of the infected would rocket. *The Human Holocaust*. I thought about leaving the house and journeying. About finding people to share what I had learned. But now that I had satisfied my own curiosity about the flesh vessels stumbling about my neighborhood, I was bored with the whole subject. I decided instead to fortify my home and continue with my original work.

****

Throughout the passing months survival became a way of life. No military came swooping in to mow down the army of vicious undead, no construction rebuilt the damage that had been done during the riots, no electricity returned, and no people moved back into the town. Well, except for one. My colleague and fellow physicist Stan Atwater had originally evacuated with his wife Brenda. They'd left to find some of her family further up in the state. Stan survived, no one else did. He then spent a period of time wandering from place to place, looking to track down his loved ones. It made me feel spectacular that I had no loved ones to look for. All of that wasted effort sounded depressing.

After some time Stan returned back to the town, not knowing where else to go. You can imagine my surprise when I heard a knock on the door. Frankly, his company was welcomed, especially since he could help me with the invention I had been constructing. Not long after Stan moved in, we came across a survivor on one of our gasoline scavenges. We found Richard sobbing on the floor of a church. After hearing a horrific tale of how Richard had lost his wife and children, we felt obligated to invite him to live in our home as well. Richard was of little use to my work, but he made a great lookout and proved to be a resourceful scavenger. He was also exceptional at killing. If this man hadn't been so morally sound and genuinely nice, he would have made a successful mass murderer. Maybe it was losing his family, his home, and his life, but he was certainly harboring a surprising dark side. It came out in his short scream bursts while he demolished skulls harboring infected brains every time we got cornered or surrounded. He could instantly turn any object into a weapon and find the quickest way to kill as many Hollows as possible.

"This is it. This has got to be it." My chest swelled with an anxious breath.

"I think you might be right, James." Stan was grinning ear to ear. We both stared at the creation that had been more than a year in the making. I'd long known that moving matter from one place to another through teleportation did not violate the laws of physics. This, of course, did not mean that I could make it happen. But I was determined to give it a try. There was something about the Human Holocaust that had made this even more important to me. I felt like this could be useful somehow, that I *had* to do this. Plus I had much more free time without all the social interactions of the previous world.

"The Hollows are active tonight," said Richard in a loud whisper as he ran down the stairs towards us. His shoes were creating more noise than his voice. "I think a couple of them know that we're in here, they're awfully interested in the place."

"Did any of them see you?" Stan asked, concern growing on his face.

"No, no, of course not," Richard said anxiously. I knew they hadn't seen him; we had everything boarded so thoroughly there was really no way to look in. Our own sight was limited to thin slits strategically placed on all sides of the house, just enough for us to press an eye up against to see outward.

"Richard, you're going to want to move," I said, positioning a can of ravioli onto the smaller of the two 'launch pads' that I had created. The larger launch pad sat on the floor, large enough fit a large crate upon. The smaller launch pad was better suited for a tabletop, just big enough to fit a miniature poodle.

"What do you mean?"

"What I mean is, you're standing roughly in the area that I'm calculating the matter will reform. You should be less frightened of brain-dead bodies staring at a house and more afraid that a can of ravioli is about merge with your stomach."

47

"I wish that can of ravioli would merge with *my* stomach," muttered Stan. I gave him an exasperated look. "What? I'm starving," he said.

"We'll eat when this thing *works*."

Richard had now moved far away from the staircase and was pressed against the wall, staring down at his stomach, trying to imagine what it would be like for an object to start forming within him.

"This is it. Let's do it." I set the dials to match my calculations to move the object horizontally about 11 feet from the launch pad. I turned the machine on and it started making a *whirring* sound. *If it works according to plan the object should disappear and reappear in the middle of the air near the stairs.* I planned to check every word on the label of the can once it reappeared, as well as the circumference, height, weight, temperature of the ravioli within, and even the taste. If it was truly the same exact can in every way, then the matter reformed perfectly and it was truly teleportation. I pulled the switch; this was to be one of the greatest moments in history. The machine grew louder and the can started to glow. It was as if the air surrounding the can was creating small flashes of light.

"Guys… It's kind of loud, they're going to hear it," Richard said, a look of anxious fear forming on his face as his breathing grew faster. I didn't care what those corpses heard. I glanced to Stan and he was entranced, staring at the can that now appeared to be vibrating. The machine grew even louder. I started to hear some strange moaning from outside, the Hollows had heard. Then, something magical occurred. The can was gone. The three of us looked towards the stairs and waited. Our eyes started to dart about the room looking for the can. We listened closely for the sound of heavy tin hitting the floor. But nothing happened. I shut the machine off and sound turned to a slow quiet 'whir' and then to nothing.

Stan walked up to the pad and waved his hand where the can once was. "The air feels a little hot… Do you think maybe it just destroyed the can?"

I walked up and felt the air with my hand as well. "No. The temperature would be much hotter than this if that entire can's matter was turned into pure energy."

"I'm going upstairs to take a peek outside," said Richard. He was still nervous about the Hollows.

"I'll join you," Stan said. "I want to double check all of our fortifications to make sure there's no weak spots."

All three of us had already checked every inch of the house today for weak spots. And yesterday. And the day before. I wasn't concerned with that. *Where did the can go?* I sat down in a chair near the launch pad, staring at it for a couple minutes, my mind trying to grasp what could have happened. The only explanation was that the can traveled much further than I'd intended. Perhaps it was out on the lawn somewhere. Or embedded in a nearby tree. I was tempted to take the risk and leave the house with a flashlight to look for the can. That would be a pretty stupid way to die though. My headstone would read something awful like "He *really* wanted to find that ravioli."

Then, just when I was convinced that I must've made some error in my math, the impossible happened. The can had reappeared on the pad. It was there, sitting in the exact same position that it was when I'd turned it on. "Stan! Get down here!"

After more tests we came to the conclusion that the further the distance we tried to teleport an item, the longer it took for it to reappear. There was only one explanation. The can wasn't traveling forward through *space,* it was traveling forward through *time*. After changing our calculations from distance to time, we found that an object sent 20 minutes into the future would reappear exactly 20 minutes later.

"Congratulations Chef Boyardee, you're officially the world's first time traveler," I whispered affectionately to the can. My eyes met with Stan's and he could see what I was thinking. We had created a functioning time machine and we *needed* to try it on a human being.

"So you think we should all go to the future?" Richard asked, clearly not listening closely enough to the conversation we'd all been having for the past hour.

"No, of course not Richard. What would be the point of that? The future could be even worse. We don't even know if there will be any future to go to. The only thing we can be confident of is the past. We know the past was safe because we lived it. I can make the machine send something backward in time just as easily as forward."

" Are you going to try it on the ravioli first?" asked Richard.

"No, it has to be a person. Just a small test, such as traveling backward one day or a few hours."

Stan jumped in, "James, this is incredibly dangerous. The human body is infinitely more complex than a can of ravioli. If the matter doesn't form right, if even a single strand of DNA is out of place-"

"I'm going to do it myself, Stan." He stopped talking and gave me a questioning look. "I'm certain. I want to do it. Desperate times call for desperate measures, and if this works we have a shot of going back and changing history."

"We haven't even tried it out on so much as a rat yet-"

Suddenly there was a flash of light from the larger launch pad on the floor next to the machine. *But it's not even on!* It was a person. A *person* was forming before my very eyes. It was *me*!

"And this is the part where you change your mind, Stanley," said the new me that had just appeared in my basement. Then Richard fell to the floor.

"Richard! What happened?" Stan ran over to Richard, who was unconscious on the floor. His eyes kept moving between Richard and the duplicate of myself standing on the launch pad.

"He just fainted," said my second self. "Kind of funny actually."

"So… You're from…" Stan understood what was happening but just couldn't seem to believe it.

"The future. This is it, the human test." My future self turned to me. "You do it in about six hours." It was incredible. I had done something that others never could, that even some of the most talented geniuses in the history of the human race could not accomplish. All those experiments in reversed causality, all those physicists wasting their time playing with protons; it was just the human race spinning its wheels. I had actually done something; *I* had actually *advanced*.

A loud smash came from upstairs, one of the windows in the living room. Richard started to come to as Stan shook him. "The Hollows, they're trying to get in!" Stan urged.

"The windows are all boarded up, smashing the glass won't help them any," I replied, walking towards the stairs. We heard more smashing, and then loud slamming against the boards. They definitely knew there were people in here.

The four of us stayed up through the rest of the night, trying to discuss time travel theories, but constantly being interrupted by threats against our wellbeing. We continued to hammer layer upon layer of boards over every possible entrance, but the infected started becoming enraged and their strength seemed to increase as they continued to pound and tear at the house. Their noise and aggression attracted other Hollows like a pheromone; even I was becoming worried. I watched Future-Me closely as he helped us repair the areas that were becoming damaged. It was as if he knew where each spot was going to become weakened before it happened. I grabbed him by the arm and yanked him aside, keeping my voice low so as not to be heard by Stan and Richard. "Tell me what your day was like yesterday," I said in an urgent manner, immediately recognizing how ridiculous that request sounded.

"What do you mean, James?" he replied, a concerned and curious look on his face.

"You can call me Dr. Roth, I don't care if you are me. You know damn well what I mean. Last night were you visited by a future version of yourself in the basement just like I was visited by you? Did you already live this exact experience out exactly as I am now, even questioning the future-you like I am???"

He stared back at me. His face grew serious, and then he simply nodded slowly and slightly.

"Then…" My eyes grew wide and I took a step backward, realizing what this meant.

"James! And other James! We need to start planning for the trip back in time," Stan shouted, as he pushed the couch up against the splintering back door. He knew it no longer mattered if the raging corpses outside heard him speak, and it was also necessary to shout as the gurgling, grunting, and bizarre throaty screeches coming from the Hollows grew louder and more frequent. "We know the exact day the infection spread. Do we know the time?"

"I remember the time," I said. "I remember the first news report took place only fifteen minutes after the first infected person was seen. And it was right in this neighborhood."

"Mother Mary," breathed Richard, as he began nailing a small table over a hole that had been broken through the boards covering the living room windows. "But – but how would we stop it from happening?"

"Well if we catch the first known infected person before they're able to spread it, we can kill them. Just like that, done." After fourteen months of living in this Hell on earth, it was obvious Stan had no problem with outright killing a perfect stranger. Especially if that meant seeing his wife again. "We'll have the advantage of knowing what the hell is going on. Instead of trying to help someone, like others tried to do 14 months ago, we'll just destroy the infected brains and end this!"

"But we don't even know who the person was, or what they look like," replied Richard nervously.

Future-Me spat back "Richard, I'm pretty sure you know what an infected person looks like by now," as he stabbed repeatedly at a hand that had emerged through the boarded kitchen windows with a steak knife. "And you, 'Dr. Roth', look at the time." He pointed at the grandfather clock in the dining room. "Time for the human experiment, you need to go test out our time machine."

"What are you talking about? We already know it works, *obviously!*" I waved a hand in the air in his general direction, my living proof standing before me.

"At this time, on this day, you do the human experiment test and go back six hours, so you can scare the crap out of Richard and make him faint and then help your past self fortify his home during this Hollows attack."

"*You* go back then!" I yelled at him.

He approached me and put his hand on my shoulder, his eyes growing serious as he talked to me slowly. *Is this what I looked like when I did this to people?* "James, I already traveled to the past, and now I'm living out my present. It's time you do the same. This is the way it already happened, so this is the way it will happen again." This he spoke to me quietly, so the others couldn't hear. "There is no other way."

"But, if this happened to you and then it happens to me, it's just a loop. As if time was already this way, regardless of the invention, it hasn't changed."

Future-me looked grave, he spoke softly, "That's what I said too."

I looked to Richard and Stan, nodded slightly, and started heading toward the basement.

"Wait, James, where are you going?" shouted Stan.

"I have to test out the time machine!" I yelled back, as I ran down the steps.

I ran through the formula in my head to convert distance to time, then fiddled with the settings on the machine. I stepped onto the launch pad and pulled the switch. The whirring grew loud and I felt light, as if I might float away. *Good luck everyone, whatever happens I'll be going through it with you again soon.* A bright light overtook my sight as my molecules dissolved and reassembled six hours earlier.

****

Stan and Richard shouted to my "past self" as he headed down the stairs towards the invention. They looked as if they were losing their friend; a look of hopelessness came across their faces as they frantically tried to reinforce the cracking wood keeping the Hollows at bay. I was busy stabbing at a grotesque hand reaching through some broken boards in the kitchen. Black fluid was draining from the wounds I was creating. You could hardly even call it blood. The past 14 months had not been good to the infected. They truly appeared like corpses now; their flesh had peeled back to show rotting muscles, their faces in a severe state of decay. It was amazing that they were capable of anything, let alone this impressive strength and rage, with how long they had technically been dead. Something was keeping the necessary parts of them active and 'alive' enough to continue their sole mission: to infect the last of us.

Stan gave me a cold look. "Why did you let him go do that? He doesn't need to be six hours in the past, we need him here right now!"

"Stan, *I'm right here!* It's not as if you lost anyone, that was me and this is me. You don't need us both. He had to test the invention, because I tested the invention, that's just the way the time stream works."

He shook his head. "But what about… What about the parallel timeline theories? You going back altered the past six hours and created a separate timeline, right?"

I looked at Stan incredulously. "Really Stan? How could I possibly have the proper evidence to answer your question? It's not as if I can *see* timelines in front me."

"Damn it, James! I'm theorizing!"

54

At this moment, we both realized there was something wrong with Richard. He had been pressing himself up against the boards over the front door as they thumped with the weight of several Hollows, but now he had slid to the floor and was on his knees. "Lord, I give up! We don't deserve your mercy, we never have! But please, Jesus Christ, my savior, I just want to be with my family." He began to sob and the boards began to crack. Stan and I both abandoned our own repairs and ran to the front door. I shoved my shoulder up against the boards as they bowed inward, cracks shooting through the wood and small shards spraying outwards. Stan knelt down in front of Richard, grabbed him by the shoulders and shook him.

"Snap out of it, man! You want to see your family again? Then we need to get to that damn time machine and go back to stop this infection from spreading! No more Human Holocaust, no more apocalypse!" Stan leaned in close to Richard's face, his voice softening as he tried to reason with him. "You'll see your kids again, your wife again, it'll be like it none of this ever happened. I promise. You can't give up now!"

I found myself thinking that after being the first human time traveler only a mere six hours before, this was not how I wanted to be celebrating. Someone should be baking me a damn cake. Then I felt the weight of a horde pressing against the door, and my physique was in no shape to match their strength. "Stan! Grab Richard and let's make for the basement, I can't hold them back any more!"

Stan began to tug at Richard by the arms, but he just flopped around like dead weight. Apparently when people lose all hope they turn into stubborn children. As Stan began to drag Richard across the living room floor, the boards snapped in half and I hit the floor, the wood and what was left of the door collapsing on top of me. I managed to roll to the side as the Hollows tumbled in, the first five or so tripping over each other and falling on their faces. The infected horde was shoving into the doorway fast and hard, creating a bottleneck backup that bought me a few seconds to free my legs from the wood and get to my feet.

Richard was still on the floor, but now staring at the pileup of writhing Hollows with wide, terror-filled eyes. His mouth began to quiver as he tried to form words; he appeared oblivious to Stan's shouts and tugs at his arm. Stan crouched down to wrap his arms around Richard's chest for a better grip and suddenly it was as if he noticed Stan's efforts. Richard looked back at him and started to sit up and scramble backward like a crab, but something stopped him from getting far. I was on my feet now and searching for the kitchen knife I'd dropped earlier when I saw the bone-like fingers wrapped around his legs. One of the infected in the squirming pile stuck in the doorway had freed himself and grabbed ahold of those legs and was dragging him back toward the door. I bolted to Stan's side to help pull Richard away when an ear-splitting shriek nearly gave me a myocardial infarction. The living corpse was tearing into Richard's legs with his teeth. I grabbed Stan's shirt and pulled him away. "It's too late Stan, the infection's in his system, *let's get to the basement!*"

Luckily I'd installed locks on the basement door, but I had stupidly not fortified it any further. After bolting it behind us we ran straight to the time machine. It had become more than our mission, it was now our escape.

"December 4th!" Stan shouted, pointing at the machine with his forefinger as if he was jabbing the air in a fencing match.

"I know, I know, 4:10pm!" I was at the machine now, looking at the buttons, my mind racing out of control.

"What are you *waiting for*?" he yelled, racing to my side.

"I'm doing the math, Atwater! If you can calculate distance to time in your head faster than I can then please, feel free!" I could already here the door cracking under the pounding thumps of the Hollows that had filled my home. "Wait... Wait!!! We have to move it over here!" I pointed to the middle of the basement floor.

"What?! Why???"

"Because I'm pretty certain 14 months ago I had that work table in this spot. I've rearranged the lab setup a few times since then!"

Stan's face changed as he realized our bodies may very well materialize inside of a piece of furniture, severing us in half. "Wait! *Pretty certain*?"

"It was a long time ago, damn it! I've had other things on my mind!" I started lifting one side of the large launch pad. "Just trust me and help me move it over there."

"The cord's not long enough, we have to move the whole machine." Stan and I lifted the invention and waddled toward the center of the floor. In between grunts I asked "What will you – *umph* – do if we succeed? I mean, about our past selves? They'll still be there too you know."

Stan's face was red and perspiring from the weight of the machine. "I don't know what you plan to do, but I'm going to kill mine. There's no way I'm sharing my wife with anyone, not even myself." I started contemplating whether or not killing Past-Stan would cause Stan himself to die, and what that would mean for all we'd accomplished in our own timeline. I imagine I could have figured it out but I was interrupted by the sound of the basement door coming off the hinges and crashing down the stairs with two Hollows lying upon it like a boogie board and two more rolling down the steps behind it.

"Oh *SHIT*!" We dropped the invention on the ground and both ran to the launch pad, lifting it in the air and moving it like highly-caffeinated bodybuilders lifting pillows. The door, and the Hollows upon it, hit the basement floor and slid to a stop about four feet away from us. I started fiddling with the dials and buttons, trying to set the date and time correctly. If I was too late by even a day then we had damned ourselves. There wouldn't be a time machine in the past for us to use again. It had to work perfectly this one time. Stan grabbed a lamp and started pummeling one of the Hollows in the head with it as it attempted to get to its feet. Another Hollow was already up and grabbing at Stan's arms. Stan stumbled backward and fell to the ground screaming *"Hurry James!"* as the corpse leaned down upon him. He was doing his best to push it away, but the Hollow was absolutely feral, shaking with energy and gnashing its teeth.

I pressed the last button for the coordinates; it was time to go. The basement stairs were full of the deceased, shoving and climbing over each other to get to us. I kicked the corpse in the side repeatedly until one of his ribs broke with a *crack* noise and my shoe got stuck within him. The front of my foot was about 4 inches inside the Hollow, wedged between his broken ribs. He looked at his torso with momentary confusion. In this moment Stan was able to shove him off of his body, which caused me to have to hop on one foot, trying not to fall over and make myself an easy dish for the hungry Hollows filling the room. I twisted my foot and yanked it out of the shoe. Stan scrambled to his feet and together we jumped onto the launch pad. I pulled the switch as Stan shoved away two of the corpses attempting to travel with us. The whirring of the invention grew loud as the air surrounding us turned to bright light. I thought of the conversation I'd had with Past-Me earlier. This timeline kept flowing just as if the time machine had always been invented. I met the James Roth from the future before I ever got on the pad myself. That being known, I felt it in my gut that this wasn't going to work; that 14 months ago a Future-Me arrived the day of the outbreak, but everything happened anyway. If this is one timeline, then what happened? How did I fail? Where did the Future-Me go? *Well now **I'm** "Future-Me", and I will fix this! I'll stop the Human Holocaust!*

Then, just like that, we were in my basement again, but there was no time machine and no horde of Hollows trying to rip us to shreds. I held my hand out in front of my face and breathed a sigh of relief; everything appeared normal.

"Do you feel kind of funny?" asked Stan, holding his head.

"I'm feeling fine," I replied. "Maybe you're experiencing some side effects from your molecules reassembling. We need to check the date and time!" I ran up the stairs and to the computer.

December 4th, 2014. 4:06pm. Perfect, I nailed it! Stan entered the room and I grabbed him by the arm. "It's about to happen! This is it, it's going to happen on this street!" We ran out the front door of the house and out onto the street.

"James-"

"Stan, we have to keep our eyes peeled. The first outbreak is going to take place somewhere around here. I'm going to head this way towards the end of the block, you head the other way!" And I took off at a jog, my eyes darting back and forth across the street, looking for anyone who might be infected.

"James!" Stan urged, sounding weak. I turned around just in time to see James collapse to the ground.

When I got to him he was lying on his side, knees drawn up and shaking violently. After a couple hard heaves he was vomiting, half on the ground and half on himself. I put my hand on his forehead, it was on fire. *No!* "Stan, what's wrong? What the hell happened?" Instead of a reply, his eyes rolled back into his head. *No!* I rolled him over onto his back and looked him over. The backside of his right hand was bleeding; I lifted it and saw 3 deep impressions in the shape of teeth. My head was spinning. *The corpse that had him pinned down in the basement... It bit him!* Stan's shakes suddenly stopped, and I looked down to see a dark urine stain growing on his pants. He was dead.

I stood up and backed away; this couldn't be true. *This was when the outbreak started.* I looked all about me but Stan and I were the only ones on the road. Could it be? I suddenly realized I had no weapon. What the hell was I thinking? I was going to stop the Human Holocaust from taking place with my bare hands? I positioned myself to kick Stan in the side of the head, but I had no shoe on my kicking foot. I started wondering how much force I could kick a head with in a bare foot without stubbing my toe and tried comparing it to how much force I could kick with my other foot at all. It was at this time Stan started moving again and I screamed in a pitch that would shame 80s hair bands. I kicked his head repeatedly with my bare foot, but he was twitching about and

I didn't seem to get any good shots at the temple. Then I felt his fingers grip my calf with a strength I never expected Dr. Stanley Atwater to possess. His fingers felt as if they were digging directly into my flesh; I tried to pull away but instead ended up falling on my back. Stan pulled himself up, still gripping my leg so forcefully that I began to shout in pain.

Suddenly I heard sirens and saw blue and red lights bouncing off the pavement around me. Car tires came to a screeching halt and I heard a man shout, "Hey buddy, get off him and put your hands in the air!" Then I was pinned under Stan's weight and felt the searing pain of teeth digging into my arm. *I think I remember hearing about this on the news.*

Damn.

About the Author

Joshua Werner

Joshua Werner is an illustrator, author, designer, and all around creative mastermind looking to infect the world with his special brand of eccentricity. He resides with this family in America's Mitten where many have dubbed him the nickname "Frantic", making his living by sitting awkwardly in a chair for long hours working his right hand until it breaks open and bleeds awesomeness out onto paper.

You can check out some his artwork at:

www.AsFallLeaves.com

www.facebook.com/AsFallLeaves

If you would like to read more of Josh's fiction from Source Point Press you can find his short story "Osiris" in the anthology "Alter Egos Volume I" and also a collection of his horror stories in "Adoration for the Dead: Tales of Insanity and Terror."

For more information on these books, visit these awesome sites:

www.sourcepointpress.com

www.facebook.com/SourcePointPress

www.facebook.com/AdorationfortheDead

Marrowbone

By Kitty-Lydia Dye

Slurp... crunch... snick...

Mila wasn't sure whether it was saliva, blood or meat juices dribbling down its face. Fat drops of it pattered onto the floorboards - if she closed her eyes she could almost pretend it was raining.

Yet, there wasn't a cloud in the sky; the sun had been shining before night fell. She'd been lazing about in that heat. Then, night had brought these creatures with it. They were more animal than human. Grunting carnivores who could never be full.

When had her father's cut started to become infected? He'd been caught in the stampede of risen corpses, had to fight tooth and nail with a briefcase, and when he had stumbled in there'd been a gash down his back.

Dripping, like rain.

Mila smelt the decay, she had known it was too late, but her mother had persisted in cleaning, endlessly cleaning that wound. Hoping the pus would stop seeping. Hoping that what she'd seen lodged in the gristle of flesh was not a squadron of maggot eggs. She'd been up to her elbows in his blood, small cuts on her skin from everyday life soaked in it. Contaminating her. Her breath and hair started to smell like rotting meat and she didn't notice. Too focused on saving her dying husband.

Then, there was the daughter, Sarah. Small, young enough to believe in such terrible things which crawled in the night, who had been promised a kiss and a story before bed from daddy when he got back from work. Daddy's mouth had gone slack, his painful moans gurgled into a death rattle.

She had understood what was happening, never quite believed fiction was fake, and so had picked her cat Mila up and gone into the attic. To hide.

The change in the human was not sudden. It crept up, as a spot growing into a pustule would. His whole body appeared nauseous, the pale anaemic tinge turning green. A crust encircled his eyes. Thick, sticky mucus, concealing the whites. The pupils did not react, they stared blindly on, no soul lurked behind there; only hunger.

While Sarah's mother tended to his wounds he grasped her shoulders in a half embrace. Using her to lift himself up. Nails scraping her skin. His name was on her lips. He kissed her. She clung to him... Then, there was a wet crunch. Her pained cry was devoured by him - everything gorged upon.

The nails were ground between his molars. Fingers snapped back, broken and nibbled. Legs picked clean, arms stripped of their meat. Sarah thought he'd killed her. Her mother was lying on the floor and everything inside of her was splashed onto the carpet. Only the head remained untouched.

The head whined between her bloodied lips. Spitting blood. She couldn't move her torn apart body. She was trapped there. Keening on the floor.

Mila watched all of this, gripping the edge of the attic entrance with her claws. Sarah stood in the shadows of the attic, she couldn't stand to look at what was happening downstairs. She cried, silently, so that the thing down there didn't hear her.

Worried, Mila crept over to her and nudged against the back of her legs. Her feline instincts told her to run and leave the girl - jump down, race past the feeding animal and escape into the night - but when someone cradled you throughout your childhood, saved you from a waterlogged cardboard box, you felt loyalty.

Sarah was still crying. Ignoring Mila. Annoyed, because they couldn't spend all night in the attic, she nipped her ankle. Her bloodshot eyes stared at Mila, the cat raised her hackles while another bone snapped in the distance.

There was a window in the room, pretty, a circle mimicking the full moon outside. A dead tree was banging on the glass, beckoning. There were dangers outside, true, but they were intangible; indirect. Downstairs there was a threat lurking, waiting for the girl to appear. Mila went to the window and clawed at it. Sarah opened it and cold air bled in. It negated the smell of cooling flesh and curdled blood.

The creature made a confused, grunting noise. Wondering where the sudden wind was coming from yet so mindless that it couldn't understand that a window had been opened. The girl was standing by the window, not moving, unsure if she should go out to meet the unknown dangers or stay here and starve. Mommy always warned her about wandering away from her and daddy, but now the danger *was* daddy.

She watched as Mila alighted upon the windowsill, stared into her eyes and implored her to follow. Her tail swished, mesmerizing. Sarah's hand reached out to find comfort in the feel of Mila's fur. The cat hissed and she started. *Get out,* Mila tried to tell her *Save yourself.*

She must had heard her. Her hands clutched the edge of the sill and she clambered over and into the weak embrace of the tree. She clung to it tightly, afraid she would fall out and hurt herself. Mila joined her and navigated her way until she could jump down into the front garden. Frightened, Sarah stumbled down after her and lumped into a bush with a pained yelp. Crying out with relief and terror she clambered out.

The cat's ears were pricked because the shriek has alerted someone. The monster in the house. With her sensitive hearing she could hear even more confused grunts and snarls. Long, drawn out, sloping footsteps as it dragged itself to the front door. The door handle jiggled; it was locked and the creature yelled in anger. Smashing its fists against it.

The icy air invaded Sarah's lungs, clearing up her fuddled mind. The reality of what had happened hit her and she wanted to weep at the spitefulness of the world. Her family was gone. She was on her own. She had to take care of herself.

She started to run away from the house. Away from *it* and the moaning corpse of her mother. She knew that she would most likely die on that night and not even see the rising dawn, but she had to fight!

And Mila was by her side.

****

Her little legs couldn't run for long. She wondered if the roaming corpses all over the world would ignore her if they caught her - surely she wasn't that appetizing? There was barely any meat on her tiny bones.

She dared not go into the nursery for shelter; afraid of the scene she might come across. There was a severed hand crawling in the gutters of the street, she kicked it away when it tried to grab her ankle and Mila pinned it down. Crushing it beneath her weight until it slumped obediently.

There were only the three of them on the streets leading into the city. The monsters had roamed to more worthwhile pickings and had left behind a husk, a bone picked clean, of its earlier vibrancy.

She remembered the drive back from school with her mum, waving to her friends who were taking the bus - with a short intake of breath she realized that they were probably dead - and the bustling shops along the street. The newsagents with the kind old lady, the nursery, a supermarket whose manager hated having groups of children in there, so many people and places. Now everything was like a shattered reflection, spit and mud and pus wiped over the glass so that you could barely even recognize it.

Sarah heard something shuffle behind her. It was the severed hand, scuttling after them. Mila arched her back and snarled, thinking it would shoot away in terror. It stopped and waited. Sarah resumed walking and it followed at a distance. The cat hissed at it one last time before trotting after the girl.

Her stomach growled, so did Mila's, neither of them had eaten since that afternoon and she was exhausted from running. Her throat scratched and ached.

The supermarket opposite looked deserted, not a single

65

shopper alive or dead. She had to shove a trolley out of the way to get inside.

There was an open juice carton on the checkout belt, it spilled apple juice all over the tiles. Mila went over to lick it up while Sarah wandered further in for richer pickings.

It wasn't really stealing... was it? Not when the person who owned it was dead and you desperately needed it? What would the undead do with crackers and milkshake?

The lights were flickering. Maybe one of those creatures had gone upstairs and bit into the wires. Perhaps he was still lying there, getting electrocuted again and again because he didn't have the common sense to move away.

The freezers had been emptied of their raw meat and frozen chicken nuggets, some of the fish fingers were gone too. Sarah didn't know if what she was stepping on was melted ice from the freezers or something else. She couldn't quite see in the muddled gloom. Her feet made a steady dripping "schuulunk" noise as she walked through the liquid.

Mila watched as Sarah came back to the tills and took several plastic bags. Then, she returned to the aisles and shoved boxes of food into them. Mila wasn't a cat who knew about human food but most of the items looked like junk food, the kind that children loved to snack on... but then Sarah paused and considered the food.

She was remembering her mother's lectures on healthy eating and knew she would probably be sick if all she ate was this. She resumed collecting the food but picked the more 'adult' healthier items - the look on her face was strained. She didn't know what to do, mum always decided on everything.

The bottles of water and juice cartons were too heavy for her to carry in bulk so she had to take the children's sized apple juices and milk. All went into the bags and she felt how heavy they were; her mum must have been a superwoman to have carried all this and the bigger bottles by herself.

... But she still died...

Sarah rubbed her eyes and knotted the bags up. Then, she

pulled down some bread, knowing it was too fresh to take with her and went to the cheese aisle.

Mila's fangs tore into the foil and plastic of the pouch of cat food and reached the salmon pate inside. For a moment she was content and had forgotten the dangers outside.

Afterwards the cat found Sarah sitting next to the cheeses, ripping bread with her bare hands, crumbling the cheese and shoving it into her mouth - violently piercing the straw into the juice carton, then she pulled it back out so she could tilt her head, put the hole to her lips and swallow it in one go.

There were fat, angry tears running down her face. Her whole body was tense from the creeping rage and unfairness of it all. She wanted to be at home colouring, not wandering the streets expecting to die. It seemed so hopeless and her anger at what had happened couldn't be bottled up.

She started when she felt Mila's rough tongue against her cheek. Mila didn't even know why she'd done it. It was something dogs did, the silly sappy things, but she couldn't stand to see Sarah cry. Grumbling lowly she settled in Sarah's lap and the girl resumed eating, calming down just so she could swallow without choking it back up.

The hand was sliding about in the slush of the defrosted ice.

Sarah hiccupped and swallowed the last of her meal. Her stomach roiled and the back of her throat tasted like bile but she was alive and eating cheese - not brains.

She had to get moving though. There were billions of people on this planet, all of whom were now most likely the undead, it wouldn't be long before one came back in here. At least she knew she could come back if she needed food again, even set up a home here if she found a good enough hiding place.

Sarah hoisted up her bags and left. The automatic doors had stopped working, she had to shove them aside to get out and back onto the streets...

****

The trio had walked for an hour before they noticed 'life' on the roads. There was a lorry, for supermarket home deliveries, turning. Someone was in the driver's seat, spinning the wheel, and Sarah almost dropped her bags and ran to it. Excited at the thought of another human.

Could they take care of her? Leave the surviving to the adults?

"Help! Over here!" She called out and put down one of the bags and waved her arm. The driver saw her. The lorry faced all three of them. Suddenly they heard the engine rev. Sarah took a step back. Then the lorry hurtled towards her.

Already exhausted, still carrying one of the shopping bags, too desperate to let go of what she'd already scavenged, Sarah was forced to run again. Panting, crying, knowing she couldn't outrun it.

The cat was even slower. The hand was clinging to her tail, using it as an escape vehicle, slowing her down. Mila couldn't keep up. She ran onto the pavement and the lorry passed by, only seeing Sarah.

One of those *things* was in the driver's seat. Loud country music was blaring from the radio; it banged its hands against the wheel to the rhythm - its bent, broken fingers flapped uselessly. There was a gear stick running clean through its forehead. When it wanted to turn it used its elbows on the wheel. Cackling, it pursued Sarah.

She fell. The tarmac scraped across her face and cut her skin. Sarah whimpered and struggled back onto her feet. Knowing it was homing in on her. She couldn't breathe. The fall had winded her. The monstrous strength of the incoming lorry could be felt in the vibrations racing down the road.

Sarah ran down into an alleyway and it had to go onto the next road to follow. For a moment it was distracted, uncertain as to where it should go to continue chasing her. For ages Sarah, Mila and the hand walked, the noise of the country music becoming dimmer as the driver took another road and went in the opposite direction.

Then the girl heard something, head tilted and straining to listen. Mila could hear it as well. Groaning. Automatically everyone assumed it was another of those creatures but then the groans turned into cries for help.

Could it really be another human?

Sarah followed it and Mila scampered after in pursuit, the hand scurried behind them.

There was an overturned postal van in the middle of the empty street and shattered glass was gingerly walked over, a tire had shot off the van was burning meters away. Someone was in there, a man. Blood was spilling down his hanging body, but he still looked... alive.

Sarah was small enough to squeeze through the window, her hands patting, searching for the seat belt. It snapped at her fingers when she released it, slinking away like a snake. He was heavy but Sarah heaved and grunted as she dragged him. Muscles tensed, teeth bared, as she pulled him from the wreckage. The vaguely formed scab on her cheek burst anew at the ferocity of her strained expression.

However, it wasn't enough. Only half of his body was pulled free and there was the sound of a horn beeping in the distance. Steadily getting closer. Panic set in. Her red raw hands slapped his cheeks, prodded him; he didn't rouse. She'd seen water being used to wake someone up on the television but she didn't want to waste what she'd managed to carry here.

So she spat in his face. The saliva was tinged with dust, mud and apple juice - he didn't even flinch. Sarah called for Mila, she looked determined.

"Scratch him."

With pleasure, Mila thought. The man yelled out when the cat's claws went deep into his shoulder and Sarah had to force her hands over his mouth before he alerted any more nearby flesh eaters.

"What?" He mumbled between her fingers. "Who? Where -?"

"You need to move. They're coming."

"Who are -?"

"The monsters." Sarah grasped his sleeve and pulled, struggling against his weight. Understanding, he finally stood up and woozily went off of the road. Mila nudged the hand away with her and a minute later the lorry hurtled past them straight through the postal van.

****

She hadn't stopped beaming since she'd found him. Infinitely happy that she wasn't the last human left. Mila couldn't really understand the appeal. He smelt of sweat, cigarette smoke and urine. He hadn't even said anything to the girl yet. She meowed discontentedly.

His post bag was still slung over his shoulder, it'd been dragged out with him. He seemed dazed, confused. As if he was trying to distract himself he took out several of the letters and flicked through them. He read out the names, then finally, "I guess they're all dead as well, if what you've told me is true." One of the names had been Sarah's mother's, she nodded despondently and he fell quiet again.

"Are you thirsty?" Sarah asked. He grunted. She got out a juice carton and one of those flimsy straws. "Here!" He drank loudly, slurping and making the carton sound breathless as air was sucked out. He kept on rubbing the back of his head.

"Are you hurt?"

"... I just banged my head."

"At least you're not dead." Sarah smiled widely, glad he was alive and that what she'd said had rhymed with his words, but then she became pensive, upset, remembering that her parents were gone.The post man chucked the carton into some bushes after he was finished and instinctively Sarah said,

"That's littering!"

"So?" He snapped. "I don't think the undead care about the

environment!"

Mila snarled angrily as Sarah began to tear up, hands grasping the fabric of her shorts as she tried not to cry. The hand was curled into a fist and it shook. The man relented.

"Look, kid -"

"S-Sarah," she sniffed.

"Sarah. I'm a little freaked out, that's all, so I'm going to be snappish. Okay?"

"Yeah. I understand."

"Good." He smiled. "Thank you for pulling me out. I'd be just like them if it hadn't have been for you."

"No problem!" She grinned in return. "But... where are we going to go? Is everywhere else full of the dead?"

"Probably, I -"

"What's your name?"

"Tom."

"What should we do, Tommy?"

He pulled his postal jacket tighter around himself.

"Wish I still had the van, we could be out of here and into the countryside in moments."

A good plan, Mila reasoned, *it'd keep the group safe.*

"But we should look for survivors," Sarah argued. "What if there are other people trapped like you were?"

"Then they'll have to get themselves free."

"But that's wrong!"

Tommy rubbed the bridge of his nose in exasperation.

"No, it's survival. Take care of yourself first then think about others. We should get supplies, find a car and go somewhere so far away the freaks won't even want to chase after us. Woods perhaps. Maybe even a boat on the ocean."

"That won't work forever," but Sarah knew he wouldn't listen to her. She grumpily petted Mila and the cat purred in contentment.

That boat idea sounded nice.

When they went back the way they'd come from, looking for a car to break into, the abandoned shopping bag Sarah had left behind was now torn open. The food she'd struggled to carry was dashed across the street. A regurgitated mess. Sarah tried not to let it dishearten her, thinking that at least she had another bag, which Tommy was now carrying.

They tried every car they came across, hoping there was one with the keys left inside. Unfortunately, it seemed the walking dead were conscious of car thieves. Tommy was getting more and more frustrated. "Should have learnt how to hot-wire cars instead of delivering post," he grumbled. Tommy didn't like the hand either, he didn't trust it. Muttering, "The first thing I'm going to do once we get a car is run over that thing."

The cat watched as, when Sarah's back was turned, the hand balanced on its torn wrist, lifted itself up and proudly showed Tommy its middle finger. Tommy rubbed his aching head and glared at it.

The hospital car park seemed the best place to try next. There'd be plenty of cars, possibly with their motors still running and a canteen for supplies. There'd be dead bodies as well, the group could only hope that they wouldn't be stirring.

There was a siren blaring loudly, an ambulance had crashed into the wall of the building. Two female paramedics were slouched over in it. Tommy couldn't tell if they really were dead or just pretending. Besides, no one could drive it now in that state, it was useless. Tommy busied himself with the rest of the cars and ambulances, Sarah watched him.

There was a flagpole there and a flag flying from it. Sarah didn't recognize what it meant but Tommy did. It had a quarantine symbol on it. He wondered what had happened in there, if it was a virus even worse than what those creatures brought... or could it be...

Tommy shook his head. It didn't matter anymore whether or not this undead sickness had originated from the hospital. Anything could have caused it. He returned to checking the cars, completely absorbed in the action.

Yet underneath the roar of the siren there was screaming.

Disturbed, Sarah ran towards it. Tommy didn't even notice until Mila went up to him, stretched and scraped down his ankle to get his attention. He chased after the girl and into the hospital but by then she had vanished.

Tommy hunted through reception and Mila went ahead. Peering into open closets and any other small places cats and children could reach. The screaming had stopped, she couldn't even use that to guide her.

There were flesh eaters here.

They were doctors, nurses and patients too. All of them seemed obsessed with the daily routine they had followed as humans. Checking charts. Administering drugs. Mila even noticed an undead patient who was shakily walking with a portable IV drip, though it no longer had any effect. One doctor leaned out of the window and had a crafty cigarette. When it sucked in the smoke it came out of the holes in its body.

The cat shuddered, felt like choking up a hairball, and wondered how exactly Sarah had managed to get past this lot.

There was a utility closet at the end of the hall, the door was opened enough for her to slip inside, and she found Sarah. Curled up and cradling a living nurse, shushing her tears.

"Everyone's dead -" The nurse began, weeping anew.

"I know, Lizzie," Sarah said.

"How could no one see it happening? Every night it would -"

"Shh- Hush. They'll find us."

Lizzie covered her mouth but her shoulders continued to shake. Sarah scooped Mila up and gave her to the nurse to hold and comfort her. Mila struggled but soon relented, the human's grip was strong; no wonder Sarah couldn't wriggle out of it.

A thin trickle of blood splashed onto the cat's nose and she twitched. There was a deep gash in the nurse's neck, it looked incredibly deep and the scabbed skin that had formed over it was mucky from dirt and dust. It smelled rancid to Mila.

How are we going to get out of here now? Mila wanted to ask Sarah. *I still don't know how you got past them the first time.*

73

"I have a friend outside, he can help up," Sarah told Lizzie, who shook her head.

"No! If we leave then they'll catch us, there's no more hiding places I can use."

"Follow me," Sarah ordered.

The cat couldn't believe the girl's daring. Though the creatures didn't seem to look at things too closely. Sarah's clothes were already damp and filthy, much like the ragged strips of cloth over some of the worse off undead. Fashion wasn't top on their priorities...

The girl had raised her arms, fallen into a sloping limp. There was so much grime on her face that you wouldn't be able to tell if she had a green tinge or not. A faint splatter of blood was on her shirt, from holding the nurse; she looked like any other undead child hanging about on the streets.

Lizzie mimicked her, feeling self conscious because there was snot and tears running down her face. She made to wipe them away but Sarah stopped her.

"It'll make you look even more convincing."

Mila was vaguely amused as she watched the two humans copy their predators and stumble out of the closet with a groan and a moan. There were two doctors in the hallway, reading charts that didn't have a single scrap of data on them. They glanced up but soon returned to their clipboards. Couldn't they smell how fresh they were?

Mila kept close to the humans' heels, keeping an eye on the doctors. So much for all those years of medical training if they couldn't tell who was dead or alive.

Sarah let her tongue loll and her eyes roll up into her head for more believability - Mila thought she was laying it on a bit thick.

They were back in the reception room in minutes, but Tommy was no longer there. There was another undead predator at the reception desk, pushing buttons on the telephone even though it had no dial tone.

It, once a she, was also blowing out a piece of bubble gum and

74

running an emery board over its fingers. It hadn't stopped to think that its decaying state might not be able to handle the constant rub of the board; it had chiseled down to the very bones and they seemed brittle, ready to crack and break off and that wasn't all. As the bubble of strawberry was formed several things jiggled in there - teeth, maybe slices of its tongue.

Lizzie had to choke back the nausea that coursed through her body.

The receptionist waved its hand uninterestedly, not even seeing them. Too busy on a phone which would never reply.

They hurried out of the door. The cat wondered where the hand had gone. It would have made their ploy a little more credible with that sneaking around them. The thing was little good when it really was needed.

Tommy was back with the cars, inside of one, he'd smashed one of their windows when he'd spied the keys on the dashboard. Mila bristled; Tommy had abandoned his search for Sarah after ten minutes without knowing that she was alright. *Stupid human.*

He was trying the engine, getting more and more frustrated as it stalled - then he actually took the time to read the petrol meter, had to concentrate and focus his eyes, and saw that it was empty. He swore so violently that Sarah slammed her hands over her ears and blushed. Tommy rested his head against the wheel in despair and Sarah went over to the window. She cleared her throat.

"Uh - T-Tommy -"

He lifted his face and glared at her.

"Where the hell have you been? Don't wander off again or I'll not follow after -" He stopped when he saw Lizzie and ran a hand through his hair guiltily. He relented and told Sarah, "... just stay close, I might not get there in time if something happens to you."

Lizzie rubbed her aching neck, she felt calmer with Sarah holding her hand. She touched the girl's shoulder when Sarah quietly nodded at Tommy's words.

"Well, I wouldn't be out here if she hadn't have found me." The nurse raised her eyebrow at him. "Not that it looks as though you wasted much time searching for her."

Tommy muttered something which no one could understand, then said, "I was searching for a car."

"You haven't found one yet it seems."

"I know!" He slammed his hand on the wheel in a fit of anger. His oil stained fingers rubbed painfully into his forehead, plagued by a headache which wouldn't die - an undead migraine, perhaps?

"The head of the hospital keeps his keys in his office," Lizzie suggested gently. "It's on the second floor."

The ambulance's siren was still blaring, there was an open window above the roof of the crashed vehicle. Tommy was intent on getting his hands on a working car, he seemed obsessed over it, it was possible that he thought everything would be okay if he found a way out of the city. Just as Sarah and Lizzie felt safer with the presence of another human being.

He climbed onto the ambulance roof and through the window, Sarah made to follow but Lizzie stopped her. "Is he... well?" She asked. Sarah tilted her head in confusion.

"What do you mean?"

"His behaviour is very erratic. Has he had dizzy spells or fainted at all?"

Sarah shrugged. "... no?"

Lizzie sighed to herself, wondered who exactly she had got herself involved with, and helped the girl get to the window.

****

The room was empty, there was a plaque on the wall of a medical award. Tommy was rifling through the desk drawers in search of the keys. Sarah helped him while Lizzie went to sit in the chair, feeling woozy from the wound on her neck. She yelped and jumped up.

The hand was curled up in the seat, Mila batted it with her paw. Telling it off for leaving them. It drummed its fingers as if it was shrugging in disinterest.

"What in God's name is that?" Lizzie gasped, searching for something to defend herself with.

"It's the hand. I think it's lonely," Sarah replied.

Lizzie relaxed but eyed it warily, she mumbled to herself, "... so long as it doesn't pinch me..." She chose to sit on the edge of the desk instead.

As they searched Sarah asked the nurse what had happened to her, though she was cautious because she was a little afraid she would get stuck in another fit of crying.

The woman hugged herself, swallowed. She glanced at the carrier bag still in Tommy's grasp and noticed the food in there. "I haven't eaten in a few days..." She began.

Tommy didn't seem to get the hint so Sarah went over and pulled a cereal bar out. Giving it to the nurse. Lizzie had a few mouthfuls before she told them how the hospital had become infested, "There were always rumors about corpses going missing in the morgue - we used to joke that it was a vampire or black market organ traders. Didn't really believe it was happening. Then there was some funny business, one of the workers was in there when he shouldn't have been. He got fired and nothing more was said about the matter." She took another bite. "Some of the younger doctors dared one another to go down there and see if he'd been cutting up the bodies. The one that went in there didn't come to the hospital the next day; we all thought he was hung over."

It was like telling a story. As if it wasn't really happening to her. She thought she'd watched a film like this with her ex. "Was he dead?" Sarah asked.

"... Undead. He came back the day after, looking awful. He didn't act like those things downstairs though, he talked and stuff. Said he had the flu. Only... well, none of us realized he was infecting the patients - how could we? He started to degrade, then the patients did as well. That was last week. Mr Garrows, that's the head of the hospital, thought it was something like bird or swine flu. They put us in quarantine, we weren't allowed back home - stuck in there with *him*. I found one of my patients feeding on another the next night. The hospital tried to contain it but it was too late. Soon everyone was starting to feel a little less okay and a lot more... dead." Unconsciously she scrunched up the wrapper in agitation.

"By yesterday there weren't any humans left. The virus became worse and it was a full out transformation rather than a steady sickness which took days to spread - the sickness evolved... All I did was hide, nothing else I could do, and then tonight they broke through the quarantine. Most of them left the hospital but the rest remained, it's like they think they're still alive!" She covered her face with her hands, finally coming to an end.

Sarah patted her elbow comfortingly.

"You're alright now."

Lizzie sniffed.

"I didn't even think of leaving this place, just expected to die any minute if I moved. I thought nothing bad would happen if I stayed still."

"Must have been hell," Tommy murmured. "It was like the apocalypse for me, and that was after one hour of it, I can't imagine having to go through a week." Even though they would have to endure a week, then a month, a year, maybe forever. He groaned and leaned against the wall at the very thought of it.

"Tommy?" Sarah asked, she touched his arm for attention. He waved her away. "What's wrong?"

"A headache, that's all." His eyes looked bloodshot, every few seconds his tongue would swipe over his lips.

Lizzie felt his forehead and peered into his eyes.

"What happened to you when the creatures broke out?"

"I crashed my van a bit before night fell, wasn't even because of the monsters. Stupid drunk driver coming home from an afternoon of boozing. I was out of it for most of the day."

Lizzie ushered the hand away and made Tommy sit in the chair. She started searching for a light she could shine into his eyes.

"Concussions are bad, right?" Sarah asked her, getting upset

78

with worry.

"Only if you don't keep an eye on it," Lizzie replied. Sarah was wringing her hands. The nurse smiled at her. "Could you go find some food for us to take when we leave? I'll look after Tommy, don't worry, he'll be alright."

"O-Okay. Come on, Mila." The girl and her cat left the two of them alone.

"I've got a penlight on my keys somewhere," Tommy said. Lizzie rummaged through his pockets, pulled out his keys and proceeded to flash the tiny light into his eyes.

"Is she your daughter?" She asked. Tommy shook his head, then winced and wished he hadn't.

"No. She saved my life though; dragged me out of the van before it got crushed by a lorry."

"She's a good kid."

He could smell the dying remnants of her perfume as she leaned over and waved the light in front of him, something lemony. Her neck pulsed with life; each breath she took made the harsh scar across it quiver, on the threshold of breaking and spurting out more blood. Her eyes seemed glazed, a white haze going over the pupil... but he couldn't really tell if it was his own eyes tricking him.

Tommy wondered who she had lost when the night fell - Boyfriend? Girlfriend? Children? He dared not ask but he knew how painful it was. The ring his ex-fiancee had thrown at him the day before the outbreak was still in his pocket.

How were they going to survive all of this? Overnight their town was in ruin - no one could escape such mindless destruction. Everything would be devoured or become one of those *things*. The ultimate leader of the food chain; the living dead.

****

There were vending machines with crisps and sweets but Sarah didn't have any money on her and she thought she might attract attention if she gave it a kicking. The canteen was on the ground floor so she had to be careful when she tiptoed down the stairs; this was where most of the creatures congregated, ready to pounce on a weary human should they come stumbling inside.

It was a small hospital, only three floors high... or perhaps they were afraid of building a fourth floor? It didn't matter, death had still come to them.

As in the supermarket the meat had been taken, all that was left was cold mashed potatoes and an array of bars and crisps. Bottles of orange juice almost as big as Sarah loomed over her. Sarah took as many bars as she could fit into her pockets, tried to lug one of the bottles and gave up. Tommy would have to come back down and get it himself.

When she returned to the stairs she found one of those *things* loitering around nearby, one of the dead nurses was making its rounds. It was getting annoying now. Would she ever be given a chance to breathe or sleep? Or would there always be the leering presence of a flesh eater just around the corner? It was like they knew where someone wanted to be next and went straight there. A human seeking pest.

Sarah hid behind an open door and peeked around it.

"Mila, distract it for me," she ordered in a whisper and Mila obeyed, darted into the closet opposite and rammed into an overturned bucket. The cat ran back to Sarah and watched with a secretive, sly grin as she saw the shambling nurse turn and tumble into the closet in search of the cause of the noise. It probably hoped it was a rat so it could crack open its skull - eating its brain would be like chewing a nut.

Sarah snuck up the stairs behind the nurse's back before it realized she was there. When she thought she wouldn't be heard she quietly called out Tommy's name. She hoped he was alright and that Lizzie had sorted out his head.

"Lizzie?" Sarah murmured, making her way to the office room. There were grunts and groans coming from downstairs.

The decaying nurse rummaged through the bleach bottles, hunting for a four legged morsel. Mila was intent on seeing it make a fool of itself for fun, thinking Sarah was alright, when the screaming started. It was a mixture of a sob and a yell.

The nurse had heard it as well. It moaned hungrily and the cat rushed up the stairs two at a time. The creature was stumbling behind, much slower in comparison. It slipped on a stair and slid back down. Sarah was still shrieking.

She was standing in the doorway of the room Lizzie and Tommy were in. Eyes wide, then they narrowed as tears welled up, the scream was steadily falling in volume into half gasps, half sobs. A steady moan of despair as she remembered what had happened to her parents. Mila looked into the room.

Even in death Lizzie's fingers clung to his neck, midway through defending herself. She was lying on the desk, hair fanned out - almost as if she was sleeping.

Except... Except...

You have to have a throat to breathe, don't you?

Tommy's mouth had latched onto her neck, like a dog gnawing on a bone. Tearing, ripping. Sarah couldn't stop staring in disbelieve. Why was he doing this? He wasn't dead!

... Or was he?

She recognized the emotionless stare in his eyes and the beginning of a slimy green crust in his tear ducts. Something internal must have happened; his heart stopped or organs failed. He wasn't Sarah's friend anymore. Another wail started up from her.

Shut up, Sarah! Mila wanted to say, though she wouldn't understand her. *That nurse is coming up the stairs and Tommy will come after you once he's finished with Lizzie!*

Where was the hand? Probably turned traitor and left. It might have even found the body it had left behind.

We need to run! Sarah didn't pay attention to the cat's hisses and meows.

Even though it hurt her to do it, the cat raised her paw and scraped hers claws across the girl's shin. She stared at Mila as if she was the enemy, then it began to dawn on her. As it did for Tommy. Realizing that fresh prey was about to run away from him he disengaged from his meal. Snapping Lizzie's stiffening hands from around his neck.

Sarah didn't even bother to try and reason with him. She screamed and raced for the stairs opposite to the one the nurse was climbing up. Mila was yowling at her to hurry up. The nurse had reached the top of the stairs. It saw the girl and went chasing after at the sight of something living. However, she smashed into Tommy when he ran out of the room.

The creatures struggled with one another, giving Sarah a chance to escape. Tommy shoved the nurse away, her already damaged skull cracking against the wall. He didn't follow her immediately. Even in his mindless decaying state he knew she couldn't leave. Sarah wondered why Tommy was standing at the bottom of the stairs and not moving.

They went higher and higher, there wasn't anymore floors though - where were they going?

The roof. They wouldn't be able to go anywhere but down. Little girls didn't land on their feet like cats could. There was a strong wind up there, Sarah was almost blown away by it. It was a long drop. Sarah edged away.

The door, which led back into the hospital, opened and Tommy shuffled into view. Being dead didn't make people patient it seemed. There was no way past him.

They were going to die.

Mila lunged. She thought she could distract him and let Sarah get away, then jump from the roof herself. Her claws were unsheathed, teeth glistening with frenzied saliva. She snapped in his face; spitting, trying to blind him.

She was too small against the heavy weight of a human.

He yanked the cat off of his face and flung her down the stairs. The world spun. Mila felt each step bang into her body until she came to a stop. Everything hurt and Sarah had been left alone with that monster. Mila couldn't get her body to move though.

Then she felt something prod her in the back, it scuttled into her view. It was the hand. Mila swiped at it weakly yet it wouldn't

82

stop nudging her. It helped her stand, letting her rest her weight on it.

The stairs looked daunting. However, Mila could hear Sarah's frightened cries. No one else would save her except for a cat and an animated hand. Together the two creatures climbed the stairs; Mila pushed it up with her head, the hand's long fingers then pulled her with it. Behind them the nurse twitched in its slumped position against the wall.

One stair, three stairs, four stairs, couldn't they hurry up?

Sarah was calling Mila's name desperately - the cat stretched her bruised and battered body as far as it would go. She didn't know if she could trust the hand but it was helping her for the moment.

They couldn't see Sarah at first, Tommy stood over her hunched, crying body. Tremors raced through her. He reached down, maybe to rip off an arm, when Mila yowled to get his attention. He turned, thinking he'd have an appetizer first, and the hand smashed into his face. It held tightly on so that it couldn't be pulled off.

Tommy stumbled back into Sarah's body and over her.

Across the edge of the hospital roof - together with the hand.

There was a dreadful crashing sound. A sickening squelch. Sarah crawled over and looked down. Would he survive a fall like that? Could death come twice?

No, Mila thought. *Not with these things.*

Tommy had been impaled upon the the flag pole and had slid to the bottom, the quarantine flag bunched beneath his body. Even from here Sarah could see his arms and legs flailing. She couldn't spot the hand. Mila meowed for attention and she picked her up. Rocking gently as she took in what had happened.

She was alone again. She'd have to rely on herself for survival. Bitter sobs jolted her whole body as she buried her face into Mila's soft, warm fur. Breathing in the scent of cat. Reassuring her. Sarah wished she was a star in the sky, distant from the chaos the world had fallen into, merely shining a light in the darkness.

She had eighty years to get used to this world. A whole childhood and adult life to live.

Quietly, holding Mila, Sarah stood up and walked down the stairs. Lizzie was still dead in the room. The nurse was grizzling in the corner as it cradled its head. She edged around it and descended the next flight of stairs, going to the open window they had gone through before.

It was as though she had lost her hearing or that she was trying to listen to a static noise in the distance and had tuned out everything else. A muggy cloud all about her body. Mila clung to her and rubbed against her neck - something wet smeared against the cat's cheek. She thought it was tears.

Sarah wobbled when she jumped down onto the car park tarmac, but it didn't stop her from walking to the flagpole where Tommy was. At the sight of her his thrashing and wails became even louder yet she didn't appear to hear him.

"I'm sorry," she whispered, not looking at him.

Sarah knelt down and lifted up the fallen flag; there was the hand. It was formed into a fist and unmoving. The flesh badly bruised, broken and leaking blood. Her fingers brushed over it and it didn't respond.

Somehow it had died.

The girl placed the flag back over it, turned around and left the hospital car park. Completely numb to her surroundings and uncertain as to where she could go.

She couldn't stop her feet from walking.

****

On the outskirts of the city there was an oak tree. What was left of an old wood that had burnt down. Sarah's energy had started to flag after her non-stop march and she had been forced to concede; stopping and sitting amongst the tree's vast roots. Watching the sky.

Mila could see the moon from here as it began its descent into sunrise. Sarah had already shut her eyes in exhaustion - no matter what she did to try and rouse her she did not wake up. The moon was bleeding, a sea of red surrounding it.

It was so cold, as though the earth itself had died alongside its people. Mila and Sarah had survived the night but what could they do now? No one was coming to save them. A girl couldn't survive this infestation forever and since... since Tommy Mila had wondered with sinking dread if she would even survive the night.

The cat could see the small wounds, scratch marks the size of an adult male's nails, on the girl's neck and her mind fooled her into thinking there was mold forming in the cuts. The skin around it was becoming the color of pond scum.

She turned back to the sky, seeing that the sun was about to ascend.

Sarah's hand fell heavily onto Mila's back and she stiffened, afraid the tiny fingers would tighten and squeeze the life out of her, but they raked down, petting and stroking her. Sarah had opened her eyes to gaze at the sunrise as well.

"We'll find them, Mila," she told her. "Other survivors like us... and then we'll take back this world."

About the Author

Kitty-Lydia Dye

Kitty-Lydia Dye is a UK based writer and artist. Influenced by horror, steam-punk, video games, Japanese manga and comic books she likes to combine these elements in her writing. She is currently self publishing her steam-punk fantasy series Society. To. Engineer. Ascension (S.T.E.A) online. Her short story, "Ms. Dawn & Ms. Moon," was published in Source Point Press' superhero anthology, Alter Egos Volume I.

Links to her other and future works can be found on her blog at:

www.thewritersclearing.blogspot.com

Second Chance

By Keri Leo

My lungs were burning. Every muscle in my body ached, but I couldn't stop. Not now. They were too close. I could hear them coming, they were hungry and had caught my scent. I needed to get out of the open. Auggie's barking caught my attention. He was in front of a barn.

"Perfect! Good boy!" I ran up to the barn doors and pulled. "Damn. The doors are locked. How are we going to get in?" Panic started rising in my chest. I needed to calm down and think. Auggie started digging in the dirt underneath the doors. "You're a genius, boy." I dropped to my knees and started digging ferociously. After a few minutes, we had made a big enough hole to crawl underneath the door. I quickly refilled the hole; I didn't know if they were smart enough to crawl but it wasn't worth the risk.

The barn was dark and spacious, but holes in the roof let the setting summer sun in. As my eyes slowly adjusted to the dark, I noticed this had once been a large horse barn. There were stalls up and down the aisle, as far as I could see. There was an exit at the back of the barn and a loft. I saw a ladder leading up into the loft and figured that would be the safest place to make camp.

I had Auggie go up the ladder in front of me, to prevent him from falling. Once we got to the top, it looked as if this had been someone's shelter at one point. There were several mattresses strewn about. "I wonder if there is any food stashed up here. Auggie, use that wonderful Lab nose of yours," Auggie looked up at me, as if he knew what I was asking, and proceeded to wander around sniffing. I followed him until something caught my eye. A backpack. "Jackpot!" I plopped down in front of it. My stomach began to grumble in hopes that there would be something inside to satisfy its hunger. Auggie looked at me expectedly, urging me to open it. I unzipped it and found some canned goods, beef jerky, men's clothes, some knives, a flashlight, multiple water bottles, and dishes. "Auggie! Food and water, this is our lucky day!" I quickly opened a bottle of water, took a few sips and then poured some in a bowl for Auggie. He happily licked it up, tail wagging. I decided to save the canned food and opened up the jerky. Ripping the jerky in half, I gave Auggie his share and then took a bite of mine. The salty beef taste exploded in my mouth. It had been days since we last had anything to eat; I chewed slowly to savor every piece. Food had been taken for granted in my old life.

I lost track of how long we had been on the run. The world had become a scary place. The dead had risen and were hungry for the living. In my old life, I had been an undead fanatic. I loved TV shows, books, movies, anything undead related. I couldn't wait for the apocalypse to actually happen. What a moron I had been. This new world was a living nightmare. I was constantly on the run trying to find a safe place to rest, find a meal, and even find other survivors. This world had made me do things, the old me could not fathom doing and deep down I was still dealing with them. During the day, the undead seemed to be less active. Maybe it was the summer sun and humidity that slowed them down. They were the most active at night. That's when finding a place to hide was most important.

I could hear them now right outside. Their moans and groans were so unsettling. I got in here just in time. Turning on the flashlight, I noticed there was a door. That might be an escape option to keep in mind, but where does it lead?

I slowly opened the door, trying not to make noise that could bring attention to me. I peeked out. There was a large pile of hay on the ground below and the horde was slowly walking past the barn. Feeling safe for the moment, I closed the door and decided to get some rest.

I flopped down on one of the mattresses and pulled a blanket over me. Auggie laid down next to me. He was my only comfort from my old life. Hugging him tightly, I gave in to my exhaustion and knew what dream was coming. I could already see the images from that gruesome day appearing as I drifted farther into sleep.

I awoke with a start and looked over to my left; my husband's side of the bed was untouched. He didn't come home. This was becoming normal for him. I wondered what was so important that Jackson was never home anymore. Shaking my head, I got out of bed. Auggie happily danced around me, he knew it was breakfast time. I laughed, "okay, let's go get you fed." He ran off down the hallway to wait by his bowl in the kitchen. I peeked in Kennedy's room. She had been really sick the day before. She was still asleep. I decided to go feed Auggie first and then come wake her up to take more medicine.

"Kennedy, honey, time to wake up," I said, sitting down on her bed. She didn't stir. Brushing her hair out of her face, I noticed she felt cold. I shook her, she didn't budge. "Kennedy?!" I said louder, fear gripping me. "Wake up." I felt for a pulse but could not find one. "No, no. no. no. This isn't happening." I kept shaking her, tears streaming down my face, "Wake up, baby." I ran to my cell phone and quickly dialed Jackson's number, "Pick up, pick up, pick up," I chanted, pacing around the room. Voicemail. I dialed his number again, voicemail. Giving up on him, I dialed 911. My call was answered with a message saying all circuits were busy. "What?! That has to be a mistake." I dialed again. Same message. "What the hell is going on?!" I screamed running back to Kennedy's room. I'll just drive her to the hospital myself. I pulled her up into my arms and began sobbing. It felt like this was all a horrible dream and I willed myself to wake up. My beautiful five year old daughter lay lifeless in my arms. Her body suddenly jerked. "Kennedy?! You're alive. Open your eyes sweetheart!" My joy was soon replaced with terror. When she opened her eyes, they were not the beautiful blue eyes of my child. They were clouded, blood shot, and dead. Kennedy looked at me and lunged for my throat. I pushed her off of me and scrambled to the other side of the room. She needs to be restrained I thought and grabbed her sheets off the bed. Just as she charged at me, I managed to throw the sheet over her and got my arms around her. She thrashed and chomped at me. I pushed her down into the rocking chair in her room and used the sheets to tie her to it. Falling to the floor in front of her, I screamed, "What is happening?!" I dialed Jackson's number again, no answer. I threw my phone across the room, stood up, and locked Kennedy's door behind me.

I switched on the TV. News alerts flashed across the screen. The dead are rising. Stay indoors. Infectious disease is spreading. I shut the TV off and stood there in a daze. This can't be happening. It's not real. I smacked myself, still trying to wake myself from this nightmare. Then I knew what needed to be done.
I opened Kennedy's door. She started writhing against her restraints and chomping at me immediately. I slumped to the floor in front of her, gun in my hand and sobbed. I was grieving for my daughter and my husband. Jackson was probably dead too. I was alone. I knew what I had to do but could not bring myself to do it. I finally realized my daughter was gone and not the abomination that sat before me. This thing wanted to rip my flesh from my bones. I couldn't let her stay like this. I flicked the safety off, cocked the gun and aimed it at her head. Tears fell silently down my face, I couldn't stop shaking. Looking at her one last time, I tell her, "Mommy loves you. I'm so sorry my sweet girl. We will be together again soon," and pulled the trigger.

Gun shots rang out in the night air. Auggie stirred next to me. I was still trying to shake myself from my dreams. Kennedy, the pain and guilt from her death hit me like a brick. It was something that had needed to be done, but it is something that I would never forgive myself for. It would always haunt my dreams. Another gun shot rang out. I jumped up and ran to the door to see what was going on. I saw a group of people running towards the barn with a horde behind them. I knew I had to help them and began dragging the ladder over to the window. While lowering it, I flashed my flashlight and yelled, "Over here!" to get their attention.

They saw me and started for the ladder. I could make out four people. One tripped and fell to the ground and the undead were on him in seconds. They tore at his flesh and I could hear them feasting on him. I had to look away before I threw up. The other three were on the ladder and quickly climbing up. Once they were in, we pulled the ladder up and slammed the door shut. I turned around to face the new comers and gasped. The last thing I remembered seeing was the loft floor rushing up at me before I passed out.

I awoke to someone patting my forehead with a damp cloth and noticed the tattoo on the person's wrist immediately. Only one other person had that tattoo. My best friend and I had gotten matching tattoos to celebrate our years of friendship. I sat up.

"Quinn!" I cried tears of joy and wrapped my arms around her. "Sawyer! I thought I would never see you again." She held me tight.

Remembering that she had shown up with two other people, I looked up and received my second shock of the night. Jackson. I jumped off the bed and threw myself into his arms. "I thought you were dead," I said between sobs. I kissed his hands, his face, and his chest and pulled him close again. He kissed my head as he embraced me. Auggie jumped excitedly around us; he was just as happy by this reunion as I was. Jackson took a step back from me.

"Where is Kennedy?" he asked looking around for her. I stared up into his beautiful green eyes and my tears spook for themselves. "Oh, god no." He pulled me into an embrace and I could feel him shaking as he was overtaken with grief. My heart broke all over again. This was such a cruel world we lived in. Jackson managed to calm himself and mustered the courage to ask what had happened to our daughter. I told him everything.

"I am so sorry that you had to do that on your own," Jackson finally said after what seemed like days, but was really only minutes.

"Where were you?" I asked, "I kept calling you," Jackson looked over at Quinn and then to the ground. Quinn wouldn't make eye contact with me either. I asked again, "Where were you?!"

Quinn spoke up first, "Sawyer, I'm so sorry. We were going to tell you, but then, well, the world went to shit."

I looked at her confused, "Tell me what?! Jackson?" I looked back at him, rage swelled inside of me.

"I was with Quinn," he answered.

"Doing what?" My fists clenched.

He looked me in the eye, "We didn't plan on it happening. It just did. We love each other."

I stared at him in disbelief. I looked at Quinn. "How could you?! You could have any guy and you chose my husband?!" Quinn looked at the ground defeated. "And you!" I pointed at Jackson. "You were out screwing my best friend while I had to shoot our undead daughter?! I needed you! You are dead to me. You're not the husband I loved. He is buried with my daughter." I lunged at Jackson and saw red. I wanted him to hurt as much as me. Before I could land my punch, strong arms restrained me. I tried to pull out of his grip.

"It's ok. Calm down. Let's go let you cool off." It was the third guy from the group. He pulled me to the ladder and I climbed down, and shot Jackson one last menacing look.

I paced back and forth, my mind wandered. All this time, I had thought everyone I loved was dead. I never thought I would see anyone again but if I did, this is not how it was supposed to be. I needed to get out of there. Feeling closed in, I ran to the barn doors and loosened the chains enough and slipped through.

The cool air had felt good on my tear stained and swollen face. I inhaled the crisp air deeply, I felt myself calm down. I thought about Jackson and Quinn. Deep down, I always knew they were hooking up but never wanted to believe it. The more I thought about it, I realized I didn't feel anything anymore. I had honestly thought Jackson was dead; my love for him was buried with Kennedy under our apple tree in our backyard. My thoughts were interrupted by the sound of the new guy slipping between the barn doors.

"Hey. Are you ok? That was pretty intense back there. I'm Lucas by the way." He smiled at me.

"Yeah, no, I don't know. I guess I always knew about them. To be honest, I just realized, I don't care. You must think I'm crazy. I'm Sawyer." I stood there and twirled my hair, a nervous habit. "I was just so angry at Jackson for not being there when… well you heard the story."

"I'm really sorry that you had to go through that. I cannot imagine what it must have been like for you," he said as he took a step toward me. Before I could resist, he was wrapping his arms around me. I had tensed at first but gave into his warmth. It had felt nice to be held again. I felt safe in his arms yet he was a complete stranger to me. The moment was interrupted by a dragging sound. I turned and saw one of the monsters head toward us; one of its mangled legs dragged behind it. A few of his undead friends followed behind.

I bent down and pulled my knife from my ankle holster. I was not going down without a fight. I ran towards it and stabbed it between the eyes. I felt the blade cut through rotted flesh and bone. Black blood began to seep out. It was sickening, but it was this creature or me. It slumped to the ground. I placed my foot on its chest, and pulled my knife out of its skull. A feeling of pure elation washed over me, I killed one! Looking up, I watched Lucas take down the other two with his gun. That noise would attract more of them to us in seconds. I looked towards the barn, there were far too many walking dead between us and the doors. "Lucas! Run! Let's try the back door of the barn!" I shouted and started running.

I pulled on the doors and remembered they were locked from the inside. I banged and pounded on them. "Jackson! Quinn! Open the doors!!" I yelled frantically. Lucas banged on the doors beside me. I turned around and we were surrounded on all sides. "We're not going to make it," I whispered, as tears slid down my cheeks. I crumpled to the ground, defeated. This was it. This was how it ended. At least, I'm not alone. I never thought my life would end so soon. Even though the world was now overrun with flesh eating monsters, I had still hoped for a second chance at life. Lucas emptied the rest of his bullets into the horde that came towards us. It was no use, there were too many of them. He fell to the ground next to me and grabbed my hand. We locked eyes; I leaned in and kissed him. My last kiss before I died. He held me in his arms as we closed our eyes and waited to feel their teeth bite into our flesh.

About the Author

Keri Leo

Keri is an avid horror fan, her favorite genre is zombies. She currently lives in White Lake, MI with her furry four legged zombie hunters, Jasper and Chloe. She is still looking for a man worthy of being her zombie apocalypse survival partner but so far the only one that comes close is Norman Reedus. "Second Chance" is her first story that has been released for the public to read and she looks forward to creating more stories in the future.

Prisoners of Forever

by Katie Jones

It's hard to sleep at night, when your nightmares now walk the earth. The memories of the old world seem like centuries ago, torn to shreds by the cold hard reality of this new strange land. A human being on this earth can feel so far away from home, or what was once home. The loneliness is profound and consumes all that is left of the human spirit. At times it feels as though you are the last person alive, all other forms of life are just forms of imagination, ghosts and phantoms of things that once existed. Or perhaps, you are the ghost haunting a new world.

****

This is how the young woman felt as she sat inside a small, rundown cottage; thick, rusted bars covered the windows, allowing her to see the sun as it began to set, spilling crimson colors into the sky outside. But the woman inside could not focus on the brilliant colors flooding the sky above. She was too busy securing the run down shack she now called home and had been calling home for months now. It was a small, wooden place on the outskirts of the remote outback. Sand and dust settled in every nook and cranny. She worked hard to pull the blinds down over the windows, keeping out the darkness and everything that lived in those shadows.

Before she could settle down for the night, she had to check the perimeter outside. She hid tears behind a warriors face, she wasn't old, no more than 26 years, but she felt ancient. She had seen things no one should ever have to witness. Her hair was cut short, shorn with blunt, rust colored scissors she'd found outside. Her clothes were worn. A once white shirt now the color of red mud and her cut off jeans were ripped, faded and stained, they hung off her emaciated body like loose fabric, her protruding hipbones poked out from underneath the fabric, a sign of just how bad things really were. She opened the old, wooden door as silently as she could, but nevertheless a slight creak filled the silent night and she reached for her shotgun, slinging it over her tiny shoulder as she moved out, well worn boots stepping into the dirt outside. This was her home, her world. A small acre of arid, desert land situated in the heart of Australia. Surrounded by wire she'd scrounged up over the years. The fence was at least seven feet high, created by mismatched bits of fences, wire and tin she'd stumbled upon over time. She knew she had to ensure it would stay secure so she moved towards the perimeter, slowly and silently, eyes scanning the shadows as daylight began to dim. In places she'd covered up holes with odd bits of tin, securing it with whatever she could find. As she made her way around the small rectangle of land, she could see them coming in the distance. Three of them, moving together, they walked slowly towards the side of the fence where she was and she crouched down and watched. Their jerking movements didn't unsettle her anymore, nor did the odd gurgles, growls and groans they emitted. The decaying flesh clinging to their bones was unsightly, even after all these years, but this wasn't what bothered her. What bothered her most was the stench, like rotten meat that wafted into the air and filled her lungs. By now her gag reflex didn't budge at this smell, but it still made her uneasy.

These creatures made a beeline towards the fence. Once they got there, they stumbled into it, pressing their swollen fingers into the gaps and trying to grip at the woman behind it. The female monster pressed her disfigured face into the wire, the rotten globe of her eyeball bulging against it and oozing black colored mucus. The males were less aggressive, some might call them gentlemen compared to the female, they stood behind her waiting, but the flaring nostrils gave away their true desires as the caught the scent of a living human.

She didn't have to shoot them, they were the only ones as far as her eyes could see and the thought that they were here made her edgy. She knew she should keep the ammunition so she kept walking and ignored the creatures as they stumbled and followed her around. The constant scrape of dead weight irritated her as they dragged their feet, losing footing whenever a jagged, protruding bone caught onto a rock beneath them.

Eventually the woman went back inside and the creatures continued to push monotonously at the fence, rotten teeth gnawing at wire until they chipped and broke. The woman entered her house, bolted the door and settled down in a corner of the shack on an old, grey wool blanket. She used a knife to force open a rusted can and began to scoop the contents of baked beans into her mouth with her fingers. Chewing slowly and using her tongue to lick at the juices sliding down her hand. Once finished, she curled into a fetal position and rested on the floor. Her eye lids were half closed, unable to allow herself to fall fully asleep.

The woman went by the name, Birdie, it wasn't her real name, but it was something she'd picked up when she was a teenager, living on the streets of a city almost as deadly as this new world. These days she was thankful to have been a street kid, she knew in her heart that if she had lived an easy life she would be dead and walking around like those things outside. Back in the old days, there were others like her and she would stumble across them frequently, but once the dead stopped dying and humans became rare, she knew the safest place was to get away from all of humanity, well, what was left of it. The jeep she'd stolen on her escape brought her to the remote outback and she still had it here with her, sitting outside. Sometimes, she would have to leave this sanctuary to drive north to the old towns that used to house others and siphon what fuel she could get and collect food as she went. The trips were getting longer and longer. She had to travel further than before just to survive and going out there was beyond dangerous.

The flickering light of dawn woke her from a tormented, troubled sleep. Birdie rubbed her eyes, moving towards the window and peering out through the blind. She couldn't see them. With some relief flooding her, she moved towards a barrel, sipping at the water, cupping it in her hands and washing the grime off her face. Today, she had to go out and with dread in her heart, she prepared herself.

Birdie took the shotgun, as well as a small revolver and a backpack filled with little more than a water bottle. She needed the room to carry what she could find. Finding her way to the rust colored Jeep, she opened the door and turned on the ignition. The familiar rumble of the engine comforted her and this old vehicle seemed like her only friend. The petrol fumes rose high into the polluted sky above her, black smoke billowing out of the exhaust pipe. In the corner of her eye, she spotted those creatures from last night moving towards the fence. With a sigh she left the jeep running, taking out the shotgun and walking towards them. Her eyes locked onto the female and Birdie took in the skinny, dead girl with lifeless, sunken eyes and black, matted hair. She shot this one in the face and the front of its skull exploded, causing the creature to fall to its knees. Its fingers moved through the earth and gripped at the ground as the black goo inside of its head splattered to the ground. The others were next and she planted bullets straight into their decomposing brains, releasing the soup within their skulls. Once, the dead stayed dead. Enzymes and bacteria within the body caused the dead to decay and bloat. Death ate away at the membranes and walls dividing the insides and caused them to become nothing but a soup, sloshing around in a silent, vessel. This was no longer the case.

Birdie sighed. Finally, she unlocked the padlock securing the chains and pushed open the gate, drove through, secured the gate again and sped off down the dirt road.

The summer heat was suffocating at times. Since the earth had become so polluted, temperatures had risen. Birdie didn't turn on the air conditioner, luxuries like this were a thing of the past. Fuel consumption came first and she had to save every last drop in the tank. She drove for about an hour before pulling up into a ghost town. It consisted of nothing more than a few houses, a petrol station and a shop. There was nothing here because she had taken everything from this place before and so Birdie drove on. The car crawled slowly through the road that took the Jeep right between the few buildings, this always made her feel uneasy, as though eyes were watching her, but she had to shake the feeling because she knew if they were watching her the growls and moans would be heard immediately.

If it wasn't for the rumbling of the engine, this place would have been dead quiet. The birds had died off long ago, unable to breathe the air here when the world had been at its most deadly, but that wasn't all. Perhaps they had migrated away from humans to a place where there was nothing more than other wildlife roaming the earth.

When Birdie had first came here, she had taken to killing wildlife for food. Sometimes the odd kangaroo had provided enough meat to keep some weight on her body, but now they were rare too. Other humans had consumed the wildlife, gone back to the roots of humanity and started living off the land again. The memory of coming across a dead boy with his head buried deep inside the gut of wallaby. Its teeth cracked and crunched through ribs and organs had confirmed that those dead things didn't just eat humans, but they consumed anything and everything in their path. Deep down they were still very much like the human race in some ways.

Birdie was forced to drive further out. She passed through two more deserted towns before coming across one she hadn't been to before. She pulled up to the side of the road just outside of the town, killed the engine and gathered her bag and weapons before heading into the ghost town by foot.

Birdie was on edge and her eyes scanned the dust caked windows of the buildings before her. The silence was deafening. She moved quietly, barely making a sound as she placed one foot in front of the other. She came to a convenience store, pushed open the door, peered into the shadows and scanned the room before slipping inside. Birdie worked quickly, grabbing things off the shelf, mostly items that were in cans or foil, things that wouldn't be holding rotten food inside. She gathered her things, slung the heavy pack over her back, causing her shoulders to sag with the weight, and gripped two liter bottles of water in each hand before moving back outside and towards the car. She shoved the items into the passenger seat, before starting the engine and slowly rolled on into the town. She pulled up to the petrol station and pumped fuel into the tank. She slid the petrol pump back into place, opened the car door just as the familiar scraping and shuffling began.

Checking over her shoulder, she laid eyes on it, just one. This was a child, barely four years old, with ringlets saturated in black, rotting blood, the fluids oozed over her forehead and into her right eye, before trailing down and onto her cheeks. The wound to her head was enormous. A gouge the size of a fist had been taken out of her skull, probably by the jaws of one of her own. The contents of her brain was nothing more than black and brown sludge sliding down her skull. She wore a little pink dress, the hem fell to just above her knees. The fabric was stained in places with dirt and blood. Her jerking walk was caused by the jagged femoral bone in her right thigh protruding through decaying, black and cheese colored flesh.

Birdie stepped back, taking the gun and aiming at the little girl's head, what was left of it anyway. Her heart beat drowned out the silence around her and the snarling growls this dead child emitted weren't even something Birdie could hear anymore. Her finger rested on the trigger and each step the dead child made closed the gap between them. Suddenly, Birdie thrust the shotgun into the car, slid her arse onto the split leather seats and slamming the door, locked it and slowly drove towards the dead girl. As she passed it, the child twisted, chubby, black fingers scraped and grabbed at the driver's door. She pressed her grotesque, crumpled, grey face against the window, black and yellow ooze smeared onto the glass as Birdie thrust her foot onto the accelerator and sped away.

Birdie glanced into the rear view mirror. The dust loomed up behind her like a cloud, but she could see a figure walking towards the girl. No, he was running. It was a male figure. He grabbed the little girl and pulled her away. She slammed her foot hard on the brake pedal, skidded to a halt before turning and slowly drove back. Her eyes fell onto the man. He was tall with long, black ragged hair. He was too fast to be one of them. His clothing was worn and shredded and as she rolled down the window, his brilliant blue eyes locked onto hers.

"What the fuck are you doing?" she cried.

The man still gripped the girl. His hands held her by the neck as she clawed at the air in front of her with dead, glazed eyes that saw nothing but a meal in the Jeep.

"Leave us alone!" the man shouted and he picked up the little dead girl, carrying her squirming body into a nearby abandoned house.

Birdie pulled up, jumped out of the car and followed on their heels. The man turned to look at her, his eyes were wide with anger, "This has nothing to do with you!" He yelled, trying to shut the old, wooden door behind him.

Birdie pushed at the door, using her body to force it open a crack, unable to let this go, "Please let me in!" She said, desperate to keep hold of the only human she had laid eyes on in over seven years.

The man sighed, opened the door and allowed the woman to walk in. He still had the child and he placed shackles on her feet. She stood, chained to a rail on the wall, pulling at the chains with thick drool dribbling over her snarling lips. Her sunken eyes looking through the two of them. The man stopped and stared at Birdie.

"What...?" her voice trailed off, eyes unable to relinquish the stare she had locked onto that little child.

"She's my daughter." said the man and his face crumpled slightly, he sank down onto a steel chair and looked up at the woman.

Birdie shook her head in amazement, "She's a fucking..." her voice trailed off.

The man's eyes blazed with anger, "No, it's still Lilly somewhere in there!"

"Why doesn't she bite you?" asked Birdie, shifting her weight from one foot to another nervously.

"Because..." the man swallowed, tears in his eyes, "because I pulled out her baby teeth, one by one with pliers," he leaned forward, offering his hand to the little girl, her grey mouth opened wide and her gums landed hungrily onto his flesh, suckling and attempting to chomp away like a starving animal. The wrinkled, grey flesh of her face pressed into his skin. He simply allowed it. The saliva trickled down his arm as her heavy snorts filled the room.

Birdie couldn't believe it. She watched in disgust as the demonic little girl furiously tried to work at the flesh offered to her. "This...this is sick."

The man looked up, moving his arm away from the girl and wiping it on his shirt before replying, "She's all I have left in this world."

Birdie nodded slowly, unable to fully understand the situation. She had never conceived, so she didn't know what it was like to be a parent, but she could see the pain in the father's eyes. His black hair had the odd streak of silver, grey hairs intertwined with the rest of his wild mane. He didn't look that old, perhaps in his late thirties.

She looked around the old, weather-board house, before speaking again, this time in a lower voice, "And you've been here all this time?"

He shook his head, "No, not all this time. We came here a few weeks back. We're originally from Victoria, but once the disease spread, we came inland. The coast is thriving with...with..." his voice trailed off.

Birdie nodded, "When did she become one of them?"

"Three weeks ago," the man choked back tears, holding himself together.

"Look," Birdie said with compassion in her voice, "I have a place that's a lot safer than here. You could come with me."

The man looked up, "What about Lilly?"

She found herself glancing at the little child, still shuffling in the corner, "Are you certain her teeth can't grow back?"

The man nodded, "You've seen them, once they lose something it doesn't grow back. Not even baby teeth." He reached for a drawer, sliding out a pair of pliers, "but I have these just in case."

"Alright," Birdie said, "gather your things and let's go!"

They chained the little girl to the back seat, binding her tight so that she couldn't get free though she struggled frantically and then left town. Heading back towards the sanctuary that Birdie had. When they pulled up, the sun had set and the headlights illuminated the little cottage. There was nothing out here at the moment, so they easily opened the gates and went in.

The man turned out to be named James and he chained Lilly to the kitchen sink.

"Welcome to my humble home." Birdie said as James sat down. They ate from cans that night and as they did Birdie watched James open a third can, grabbing fists of cold spaghetti in his hands and feeding his demented daughter.

"You're wasting food." She murmured.

James looked up, wiggling white worms of spaghetti sliding through his fingers as he spoke, "She might die if we don't feed her."

"She's already dead." Birdie muttered.

As messed up as the situation was, Birdie was grateful to have another human being in her life again, that gaping hole inside of her chest seemed to be less painful tonight. As she curled up on the floor, with James nearby she tried to sleep, but the constant shuffling and moaning of the little girl was torturous to her mind. The fact that she had one of them inside of her home was terrifying.

Halfway through the night, Birdie found she had to give up on sleep altogether and she decided to do a check of the perimeter. She walked silently past the dead girl, the gargling noises she made didn't seem to bother James. He slept peacefully on the floor.

Outside, Birdie noticed that when they'd been asleep something had tried to tear holes in the wire, she scrounged around for tin and boards to patch it up. Eventually, she was happy with her work, but something about it was nerve racking. What was the point of keeping them out if they already had one in here?

She peered through the darkness. It was quiet and still. The cool breeze gripped at what was left of her hair and whipped it around wildly. Eventually she settled back down on the floor of the shack and lay there until morning.

"Good morning, Birdie" said James, leaning forward and tending to little Lilly as she spoke.

Birdie wiped her eyes, glancing up, "Morning."

The little girl was snapping at her father with her gums, smacking her lips together as though he was nothing more than a platter ready to be served.

"How do you put up with that?" asked Birdie.

James didn't even look up as he spoke, "You get used to it."

Pulling back the blind, Birdie did her usual check outside. Her eyes bulged with fear as she caught sight of the mob hanging around the perimeter.

"Holy fuck," she murmured.

James came over, frowned as he moved and peeked through the blind too. His body brushed against Birdie, causing her cheeks to flush slightly, "Where did they come from?"

"This hasn't happened before, not this many. There must be twenty of them out there." Birdie exclaimed. She turned to look at James, "Did they follow you?"

James shook his head, "We've bumped into a few, but Lilly and I are usually on the move." He paused, glancing back at his daughter, her moans were growing louder now and the mob outside were still pressing at the wire, pushing on it at random places.

105

"You fucking liar," Birdie cried as she stepped back from the window and stared at James with wild eyes, "They followed her don't they!" she shouted, pointing at the chained creature in the kitchen.

Lilly was throwing her weight against the chains now and the old sink was creaking in agony.

James looked at her. Tears welled in his eyes "I'm sorry Birdie. You know I can't give her back to them."

"What do you mean?" she cried. Her palms shoved into James' chest hard, pushing him back suddenly "You took her?"

With a shocked face, James stumbled backward, before speaking, "I did."
Birdie whirled around, staring at the girl, "Is she even your daughter?"

"Biologically, no." James moved forward, blocking Birdie's path and stopping her from moving towards Lilly, "I found her like this and I couldn't leave her."

"You idiot" Screamed Birdie as she grabbed the undead child frantically, "You have to give her back."

James gripped Birdie's wrists, holding her still with his hands. "Never, I love her like my own child."

The mass of bodies were pushing up against the wire outside now, working as one, their weight began to force the wire to bend and the steel to warp. The noise was deafening as the constant growling, snorts and groans filled Birdie's world.

She slumped in James' arms and looked up at him helplessly. "I know you've been alone. I have too. I realize you took her because you wanted someone. Anything is better than being alone," Her words were rushed and her voice was urgent, "but James, she's one of them and they will stop at nothing to get to her, to get to us. I don't know how they followed her, but she has led them straight to you, straight to me."

James stared at Birdie, eyes welling with tears as they began to roll down his face.

106

"Please James, let her go. Stay with me." Birdie cried out over the noise around her.

James glanced over his shoulder, Lilly was distressed. She threw her weight furiously against the chains. The kitchen sink was still groaning as she did so. Suddenly, her left ankle snapped, collapsing slightly as the tibia and fibula bones tore through the dead, grey skin.

"Quickly, we have to get out now, while we're still alive!" Birdie yelled.

The kitchen sink came off the wall and the child began to drag herself closer to James, stumbling on her broken ankles. Her dead hands grabbed at his clothing and tore strips off his shirt. She sunk her toothless mouth into his hip, chewing feverishly. James placed a single hand on the little girl's neck.

"I love you, Lilly." He said before yanking himself free from the child's grip and taking Birdies hand. They dashed to the door and grabbed the bag of goods, the revolver and the shotgun as they went. They jumped into the car and turned it on. Birdie backed out and pulled the car face to face with the gate. The mob was thick with dead, rotting flesh and grotesque bodies, snarling faces ready to greet them.

Birdie turned to James, handed him the shot gun and gripped a revolver in her hand. "Shoot!" She said, as her foot hit the accelerator.

The Jeep burst forward. The bulbar collided with the gate. The chains snapped and the fence exploded open sending bodies flying in every direction. Birdie drove with her foot flat to the ground. Bullets launched into the air before her and exploded into the faces and skulls of the creatures. The car crashed into some, their faces hit the windshield and caused the glass to crack. Black, brown and red flesh smeared and streaked its way over the windshield. James shot too, blowing giant holes into the skulls of some and the guts out of others. Hands gripped at the doors, open mouths pressed to the windows and revealed thick black tongues and jagged teeth.

James and Birdie left the sanctuary behind in a cloud of dust. As they drove, Birdie reached out and placed her hand into his, whispering, "We'll be okay."

****

They made their way along the road, leaving the place Birdie once called home. Finally, they came to a stop at a small, deserted town. Exhausted, Birdie set a blanket on the ground, curled up and slept.

When Birdie woke up, she found herself bound at the wrists and ankles, Terrified she tried to sit up, struggling against the restraints, but was unable to. Her wide eyes locked onto the face before her. James sat nearby smiling.

"What are you doing?" Birdie cried, terror gripping at her heart.

"Making you mine." He said and leaned over. He clenched a large rock in his hand before he raised and slammed it into Birdie's skull. Everything went black.

When Birdie came around, the agony in her head and mouth was insane. She gargled and spluttered as she spit out thick wads of metallic blood. James moved her head, allowing her to vomit the gunk out of her mouth. She tried to speak, but the pain was too much and her voice slurred. Her body shook.

James sat back as he watched the bound woman. Blood leaked from her mouth and trailed down her chin in black and red puddles, coagulating in thick clumps on the ground. He wiped the blood off his own hands, setting the pliers on the table beside the pile of teeth he had extracted from her gums. Some had been pulled clean out, tiny roots curling up from the tooth itself. Others were broken and chipped. James picked her up, Birdie sagged in his arms like a dead weight, tears slid down her face and saturated his arms. He placed her in the back of the car and drove back to the sanctuary.

Once there, he grabbed her struggling body. Birdie wriggled and squirmed, but the blood loss had taken its toll on her body. He dumped her nearby, sitting in the car and watching as what was left of the mob began to move towards Birdie. Her screams echoed through the night as they sunk jagged, rotten teeth into her flesh as they crouched over her and pressed their demonic faces into the caverns they had created. Lifting their heads every once in a while to reveal wrinkled faces smeared with blood and hungry mouths chewing strips of red, raw meat. He got out of the car, closed the door gently, and walked over. Before placing a bullet into the two dead guys eating his friend. She whimpered on the ground, a large chunk of flesh had been devoured from her belly which left a gaping hole in her abdomen. Glistening, wet, sausage like intestines leaked from the wound, perforated in places and her own feces leaked out and onto the dirt. James simply watched on as her skin began to turn a sickly pale grey and Birdie slipped into a coma.

James collected the shackles from the sanctuary and attached them to the dead woman's ankles, before placing her into the car and driving off.

This was his new Lilly. He knew once she had transformed she would be with him forever.

About the Author

Katie Jones

Katie Jones lives in Australia and spends her working days caring for people with a disability. During her free time she enjoys writing and reading whenever possible. You can contact Katie on twitter: @misskatejones89 or facebook.com/MissKate

Fair Share

By Rebecca Snow

I scratched the ragged tip of the pencil across the empty square, marking a light gray X on October 31st. Life had been tough for everyone since the outbreak; more challenging for some than it had been on my sister Lizzie and me. We had each other, but overall, it had been worse for us kids. Most didn't mind giving up school, but giving up biking or football practice was a different story. Being carted off to the secured YMCA if they lost their parents was worse. From what I'd heard, the orphans had to stay in the emptied indoor pool. I wasn't about to let that happen to Lizzie and me.

Dad gave me an XBox two years ago when I turned thirteen, so I was used to being indoors. Lizzie didn't mind staying in the house either. She was allergic to everything that bloomed, so she avoided being in the open air more than I did. But after I'd promised to give her half the haul, she strapped on her pollen mask, hid it under a bridal veil, and helped me gather supplies.

Lizzie found a box full of old, mismatched sheets in the basement. I'm not sure what Mom had been saving them for, but since we hadn't seen her in weeks, I didn't think it mattered much. I found some duct tape and rope in the garage. We'd had to cut open a difficult bag of chips the night before, so I knew the scissors were still on the kitchen counter. Placing our materials on the living room floor, we got to work. Lizzie was closer to the right size, so I used her head to mark where her eyes would be under the sheets. She squirmed some, so they weren't all even. Once I'd marked them, she used the scissors to cut the holes.

"Charlie, do we need to make mouth and nose holes too?" Lizzie asked.

"No. Just do the eyes," I said. "I don't think cutting mouths would be a good idea."

She finished snipping the sheets and flung herself up the stairs without a word. I went into the kitchen to get a glass of water. When I came back, Lizzie had returned with a tube of our mother's reddest lipstick. With her lips puckered and painted, Lizzie kissed a sheet below its set of eye holes.

"Even if we're not cutting holes, I think they need mouths," she said smiling up at me with lipstick-smeared teeth.

Smiling back, I grabbed a marker from the coffee table and made two black swirls above a lipstick mark.

"How about a mustache for this one?" I said.

"And some big, bushy eyebrows for him." She snatched the marker from me.

After scribbling the eyebrows and adding giant eyelashes to another, she rolled over in a fit of laughter.

Once she'd regained as much composure as an eight-year-old could manage, we went into the backyard. When we had been going to school, we'd been lucky not to have to ride the bus. We'd been even luckier not having far to walk. However, when we wanted to play hooky, we weren't so lucky. Our teachers were so close; they'd bring our homework to us after school.

I opened the tall, wooden back gate and looked onto the school's playground. The bodies milling beyond the chain links bobbled back and forth. They'd been there since the whole thing had started. No one had picked them up from school and if someone had come for them, the ones that came were trapped with them. We were lucky; we just ran home.

The closest ones were wandering around the swing set. They didn't have the coordination to swing anymore, but they shifted weight from foot to foot as if they were waiting for someone to free up a swing.

"Pssst," I said trying to get their attention without attracting the rest. "Hey, over here," I library whispered.

Joey was the first one to notice me. He used to follow me around the neighborhood back when things were normal. When he turned toward us, the four others near him turned as well. I glanced to the other groups, but they hadn't noticed my disturbance.

As the five shambling creatures made their way to the fence, Lizzie and I prepared. We knew that if they made any noise, we'd have to run back through our own fence to avoid the mass of bodies. We held the duct tape strips, sticky side out, at arms length.

Joey jerked within reach first. Lizzie, standing on top of an upturned cat litter bucket, smacked his mouth shut with the first strip tangling the sticky side in his hair. He wobbled in place as if he were in shock. I taped three of the others as Lizzie taped the littlest one.

"Can't they bite through the tape?" Lizzie asked as I hauled the first one over the fence.

It was lighter than I had expected.

"Nope. Not if it's stuck and we get their hands done up before they figure out how to rip off the tape."

She had gone back through our wooden gate and was luring our catch into the enclosure. When I picked up the last one, I looked up to see more of the bodies ambling toward where I stood. We'd been spotted. It wasn't a big deal though. I just carried my squiggling cargo through the gate and shut the fence. Once we were out of sight, they would forget all about us. They always did.

When I put the thing on the picnic table, I turned to see Lizzie playing a game of dodge ball with the others.

"This is fun," she said as she hurled the rubber ball at Joey. "Why don't we do this more often?"

The ball made a hollow rubber sound as it ricocheted off of Joey's head and bounced into another's face. The second one Lizzie hit teetered and fell to the ground.

"Because it isn't safe to play with them," I said.

"Why are we doing this then?" she asked as she reached for the ball with her fingertips. She bounced it twice before aiming it at a new target.

"You know why," I said taking the ball from her and tossing her the roll of tape. "We're running out of food, and I think this might get us enough to last until the Christmas cookies come."

She tore a length of tape from the roll and wrapped the closest reaching arms together. She wound the tape around the outstretched arms until one end was up to an elbow.

"Can I tape their mouths some more? You know, just to be safe," she said with her head cocked back at an odd angle as if scrutinizing her work.

"Let's wait until we know we have enough tape for all of them," I said rolling up another set of arms.

I surveyed the yard and let out a snort. Another of our captives had fallen and was wallowing in a pile of leaves, unable to rise.

"Maybe if everyone had been taped, Mom would still be here," Lizzie said.

She brushed a stray hair out of her eyes and stared at me looking just like Mom had when telling me that I would have done better on a test if I'd studied. I stared back and shrugged.

"Are you sure it'll be safe to go out tonight?" Lizzie said changing the subject.

"You know they've gotten most of them secured now, right?" I said.

Lizzie nodded.

"And they don't move far when the sun goes down," I added. "Unless you force them to move."

Lizzie nodded again. She had looked down at her shoes as if she were embarrassed that she'd seemed afraid.

"Don't worry, Liz. Just help me tie these knots."

Seeing how well the ground was securing our quarry, we pushed the others over next to the grounded ones. Dragging them to what we thought would be a good walking distance, we began to tie the black rope around each left ankle. We stood them up and inspected our work. They shuffled and bumped into each other like billiard balls in a cardboard box, but they seemed to be stable. Lizzie went into the house and came back with the sheets.

"Ok, just drape them," I said trying to get the eye holes to line up with Joey's eyes. "Like this."

Lizzie draped a few and I finished. For a final touch, I had gone into Dad's closet and taken five of his neckties. Since I'd never tied one for real before, I just did what I remembered hearing Dad chant in the mirror before his date nights with Mom: a bunch of overs, unders, and arounds.

"I didn't know you could do that," Lizzie said admiring my knot work.

"I call it the Stemple knot." I winked at her as I tightened a blue polka-dotted tie.

"You named it after us," Lizzie giggled.

I smiled down at her and patted her head as she dodged a swaying body.

"You should get ready while I finish up here. I'm guessing from the veil, you're still going to be a bride?"

She shook her head and fled up the stairs.

"You'll see," she called from the landing.

I heard her door slam as I picked up the cloth grocery bags from beside the refrigerator. The straps were long enough to hang over the ghost heads without sliding down their backs. Everything had to look right or my plan wouldn't work. We'd been warned not to play with the infected, but I knew from reading all the blogs and news reports online that if you didn't get a bite, you were safe enough.

I tied a lead rope around Joey's waist for Lizzie to hold in case our charges had to be pulled away in a hurry. In preschool fashion, I tied another rope around the last in line. That would be my safety line if they tried to gang up on Lizzie.

Lizzie's door squeaked. I looked toward the stairs and waited for her to emerge. Heavy footsteps clomped down the from the landing. They didn't sound like Lizzie's. I grabbed the scissors from where we'd been cutting sheets on the floor and backed into the darkest corner in the room.

A huge, weird shadow shifted on the wall. I was ready to scream when Lizzie jumped down the last three steps and into the room. She had the vacuum strapped to her back over a pair of Dad's coveralls. The sleeves and legs were rolled up to at least half of their usual length. She was wearing goggles and had her hair spiked up with some sort of gel. A pair of Mom's gardening boots had made the clomping footsteps.

"Who ya gonna call?" She shouted. I stared.

"Don't you like it?" She asked dropping the vacuum hose and frowning.

I took a breath."No, it's great." I smiled. "It's really great. Really creative. Good job."

She raised the hose again and smiled back. "I just thought that since we had all these ghosts," her voice trailed off into silence. Looking around the room, she added, "where did they go?"

I tilted my head to listen. There were shuffling noises in the kitchen. Peeking around the door frame, I saw our group of ghosts tangled in a ball on the tiles.

"Oh, this should be fun," I said and set to work untangling them.

When I finished, I handed Lizzie a grocery sack and the end of the rope and held the front door open for her.

"All set?" I asked.

She seized the sack and the rope in one hand and saluted me with the other. I settled a cap on my head and took up the metal bat I'd used in little league as we stepped into the chilled October air.

The leaves crunched under our worn shoes as we hobbled down the street. It was hard to see the black rope that tied them together, ankle to ankle. I was shocked that more of them didn't trip, but they marched in front of me in a shuffling step as they followed Lizzie's lilting laughter.

"Trick or treat!" she screamed into the night as we set off with our captives to fool our living neighbors.

About the Author

Rebecca Snow

Rebecca Snow lives in Virginia with a handful of antique cats. Her work has been published in a number of small press anthologies and online. Find out more about her and her work at: cemeteryflowerblog.wordpress.com

on Twitter @cemeteryflower,

and on Facebook (look for the bloody handprint).

Livid

By Scott B. Smith

"Rage, rage against the dying of the light." --Dylan Thomas

Thomas Packer's eyelids felt as if they were being pried apart as he slowly opened them. The slips of skin quickly retraced their course once, twice, as Thomas tried to make sense of the world. His mind was foggy and clearing it seemed as if he was pushing a rusted engine into service again, the parts unwilling to turn without stuttering and scraping.

Despite the movements, he wasn't convinced he'd opened his eyes at all. He was in a darkness just as impenetrable as the shadow of his closed eyelids.

Where? Where am I?

The confusion was nothing new. Over the past six years, he'd gone from occasionally forgetting where he'd put his keys to not recognizing familiar locations on a regular basis.

He tried to focus on the last thing he remembered. *I was in the hospital with pneumonia again. Pretty bad this time. The kids… all the kids were there, I think. The preacher, too.* He smiled, the muscles in his face tight as they created the almost-forgotten expression. *That sure was nice of them. I was in the hospital bed….*

He realized he was lying on his back. *Am I still…?* The tendons along the backs of his hands curled his long, thin fingers, sliding rough fingertips over the surface beneath him.

Cloth, Thomas realized. He pushed his palms down and the fabric compressed gently, rebounding slowly as he released the pressure. *A mattress. I must still be in the bed.*

The flicker of comfort this thought brought was quickly pushed aside by another bout of uncertainty and a sliver of fear.

Why is it so dark?

His right hand jerked away from his hip, reaching to find the bedside button to call the nurse.

His knuckles rapped suddenly against more of the same cloth he'd felt beneath him.

Must have pushed the sheets over the railing, he reasoned. Thomas pawed at the fabric, trying to find the hard plastic panels beneath.

He pulled and tugged, searching for a path through the sheet. After a moment, his movements became more desperate as a cold fountain of worry appeared in his stomach and began spreading outward into his body.

It has to be there, he thought frantically. *Has to be! Where else-?*

He began to roll right, intending to give his lost right hand some help with his left. The simple movement, made countless times in his own bed, came to an abrupt end as his left shoulder thudded into something inches above him. He rolled back.

What- what is-?

Both of Thomas's palms went on a hesitant search of the inky black above him. The lingering anxiety spun in his abdomen, as he began to fear his hands would confirm what his shoulder had found.

His skin pressed against quilted cloth, only inches above him. *How? What? Oh no.*

The cold, twisting emotions in his torso shot outward, consuming his limbs. He felt as if he was falling, somehow being pulled into the fabric beneath him.

No, no, no! He pounded the heels of his hands against the surface above him, the strikes growing more rapid and forceful. He kicked downward with his feet and reached left and then upward, a passing hope compelling him to look for another way to move. His shoes padded into the same cloth. His scrabbling hands found it above him; to his left. It was all around.

He slammed his fists into the top of the enclosure, stomping at the portion beneath his soles. The small space made each impact a muffled thunderclap, strung together in a cacophony of thuds. Thomas seemed to be throwing a tantrum, emotions spurred by desperation. The noise of his thrashing pressed in as closely as the walls. It was suddenly very hot. He opened his mouth to let out a cry for help.

A deep snap occurred just to his left, startling him. He froze, the sound of his blows ending so quickly he easily made out the tinkling of metal that followed.

He groped along the left wall, trying to locate the sound's source. *Nothing. Nothing but this fabric!* Frustrated he punched his right hand against the top of the space.

With a rattle, the overhead portion moved. Shocked, Thomas drew back and fell still again. He stared upward into the darkness in uncertainty. *Was… was that my imagination?* He timidly reached up again, carefully pushing against the enclosure's top.

The barrier responded, moving upward with his hand. His face stretched into a smile again. *I think… Maybe I can get out!* With a surge of relief and renewed hope, he pressed harder.

Soft metal ground against gritty stone after only a few inches. Thomas's optimism faded as the resistance grew and the forward motion ended. Finally, he stopped pushing. His arms flopped back next to him, despair crashing over him in a wave. His head lolled to the right, eyes closing.

Thomas felt air from outside his prison flow in, less burdened by heat and moisture. It moved over his skin in convective eddies, breaking through the depths of disappointment. He hadn't noticed how high the enclosure's air temperature and humidity had been until he had something to compare it to.

He laid still, not sure how much time was passing in the silent, darkened rectangle. His thoughts slowed, becoming muddy again. Memories stirred to the forefront of his mind only to sink again. His wife of forty-six years, Laura, lost not long before his mental health began to fail. His children, his grandchildren, all playing in his front yard, each becoming unidentifiable from the rest as the recollections doubled back on themselves.

What's going on? Where am I? How... how did I get here? Where is here? His hands spread out from his sides, sliding up the slick cloth beside him.

It's like I'm in a box or... or a coffin.

His eyes flew open as terror broke through the whirlpools of his mind. *They can't- they can't think I died!*

His limbs flailed out again, pounding at the sides of the enclosure.

I'm not dead! I'm not dead! God, help me I'm not!

Scratching fingers pulled the fabric away from the lid, stamping feet hammered at the casket's end.

Help me! Somebody has to help me! Get me out! HELP!

He pulled air into his lungs. A despairing moan welled up at his center and flowed out of his mouth. The casket's lining absorbed most of the sound, but some escaped to echo in the surrounding vault.

I'm not dead! I'M NOT!

The thought of dying alone, buried alive, unable to call for aid to anyone on the other side suddenly incensed him. Hot anger moved through him, blazing through the icy grasp of fear. It left behind no thought, his body running on enraged instinct.

He placed both palms on the casket's lid and pushed. Metal creaked and slowly bent, causing the entire enclosure to shudder as the lid pushed at a snail's pace upward. Thomas continued, his hearing muffled by the high-pitched noise of anger that filled his ears.

His ire receding, he pulled another lung-full of air into his body again and let out a guttural, defiant moan. He fell back into the casket's lining in a heap, blinking.

Composing himself, Thomas tried to piece together what had happened. He ran his hand slowly over the casket lid and felt, even through the fabric, how the smooth metal had buckled into jagged ridges along the center. He reached left toward the source of the moving air he'd felt earlier and jumped as his fingers unexpectedly slid into empty air. His knuckles slowly bent around the edge of the lid, hands clambering up and down its length to test the dimensions of the hole. He soon realized the gap ran down the length of the casket.

Bewilderment set in again at these new finds. *I moved... the whole lid? Did I... did I bend it against the grave vault? How? Adrenaline? Could it do that?* He chuckled inwardly. *Maybe the kids got a cheap casket.*

His eyes widened as a thought bubbled up. *Better hurry up. I'll run out of....*

Thomas put his right hand over his chest, feeling the fabric of the suit coat he wore for the first time. The bone and muscle lay completely still.

He realized that, since waking, he'd only inhaled twice.

I'm... I'm not breathing.

Horror spun in his core and reached out to his extremities like a strengthening maelstrom.

Somehow, I'm not breathing! But I'm alive. Oh, God. Oh, God!

The world suddenly felt shattered, as if each of his senses was seeing only a part of it. Panicked, he sucked in another draught of air to scream, but the action only reinforced the awareness of his situation.

As his chest rose, a small object brushed against the hand on his chest. Focus returned at the touch of the cool metal. His mind desperate for a distraction, his fingers traced its outline almost automatically.

My cross. His nerves settled for a moment. *One of... one of the grandkids gave it to me.*

His thoughts drifted from the faces of his grandchildren to the religion the jewelry represented. He thought of going to church, the events he'd attended, the baptisms and the funerals. He thought of his children's weddings and his own. He could see Laura's face clearly, even behind the veil she wore. He remembered how her eyes and earrings sparkled in the sunlight, though he couldn't recall what the earrings looked like.

Thomas remembered bits and pieces of sermons, the words and the ideas behind them floating by in his mind like leaves down a stream.

Wait… Maybe… maybe I'm dead… but alive, again. Maybe this is the Rapture? Giddiness burst through the surface of his despair. *That would explain all this. My new body's given me the strength to do this. And it doesn't need air!* He reached up suddenly ecstatic, and began pushing again. *It's time to come home. It's time to meet the Lord! It's time to see my Laura again!*

In all his years of work as a carpenter, then a steel mill worker, Thomas had never pushed harder than he did then. His anticipation and rising joy pumped through his limbs like a warm honey, lending him strength and endurance such as he'd have never believed.

The casket lid gave off a constant screech as it crumpled and scraped over the concrete of grave vault. Thomas began forcing the covering to his right as well as upward. His hands moved slowly clockwise as the lid bent to the side.

After a few moments, he replaced his hands directly above him. Under his right palm, he felt the cloth and metal of the casket lid, but his left now rested on the rough concrete of the interior of the vault's top.

Thomas renewed his efforts, the happy expectations still running through him. Despite the exertion and the press against such sturdy materials, he felt no pain in his muscles or joints.

Why should I feel any pain? He thought. *This is my new body. The one I'll have in Heaven!*

Soon the casket lid was out of his way and both hands strove against the vault. The force caused the concrete to begin crumbling under Thomas's hands, and he could feel grainy dust and tiny pebbles falling between his fingers. The debris settled on his chest and hit his face, but he paid it little mind. He felt cracks beginning to form in the surface, and his jubilation was softened by a twinge of worry that the structure might not hold together.

Soft taps, here and there, reached his ears, as the earth seeped into the space around him as the lid ascended inch by inch.

Thomas felt the fractures around his hands widen and spread. *Not much further. Hold together,* he urged the stone.

He heard a ripping sound that he mistook for the casket's cloth being torn apart. After a moment, however, he realized it was the roots of the grass above snapping, dozens of times over, as he moved the topsoil.

Almost there. He kept pushing, bending up at the waist as a bit of space opened.

Almost there.

Soft, loamy dirt began drifting down onto Thomas as the splits in the vault lid grew ever wider.

Almost there.

Light.

The blue-white glow appeared through the soil as Thomas pushed through the final layer of the grave. Relief mixed with joy, heightening both sensations. His pupils dilated painfully as they became reacquainted with the brightness above.

Almost there. Hallelujah!

The glow intensified. Cold air rushed in, pushing out the stale, warm air of the grave.

The weight of the earth had nearly overpowered the vault's lid, the dirt rushing into the growing fissures. With a final heave, Thomas pushed it aside, throwing open his tomb.

He opened his eyes again and the night sky looked down on him. The stars punctuated the darkness that was all too much like the one he'd just left. He shuddered and looked away.

The bluish halos of metal street lamps lit the hilly graveyard around him. The white tombstones and burial markers stuck out of the uniformity of the manicured green grass, the stone stark even in the light of the half-moon. The deep black asphalt of pathways, each just wide enough for a single car, bisected the cemetery in a jumbled grid. Here and there, the silhouette of a tree could be seen as they stood sentinel outside the street lamps' glow.

As he took in his surroundings, movement caught Thomas's eye beneath the shadows of an old elm several hundred yards away. The ground near a cross-shaped tombstone erupted and he could make out a form pulling itself up.

I'm not alone here! He thought, a grin pulling back his lips. He attempted to throw his right hand up to wave to whoever this newcomer might be.

His arm rose slowly, tenuously. The limb felt as if he were moving it through a viscous fluid rather than open air. Shocked, he looked over at his hand.

Earth covered the black wool threads of his suit coat, but this wasn't unexpected. His hand was likewise dirty. But Thomas's eyes grew wide at the shriveled skin, yellowed as ancient paper, pulled so tight over the tendons and bones the flesh might not have even been there. Filth encrusted his long fingernails in a brown patchwork.

Thomas's heart sank from the height of happiness. *Wha-what?*

As his hand rose slowly in response to his last command, there was a wet pop at his elbow and he felt something snap under the skin. There was no pain, but his arm fell limply back as gravity outmatched the flesh.

His head lolled to his left, and he looked down at his other hand, which was in much the same shape.

What is this?

Looking back up to the silhouette he'd seen before, he saw that two more had pulled themselves from the ground, while another was crawling on its belly over the side of a grave. The first figure staggered slowly out into the light of a street lamp.

It was something from beyond Thomas's nightmares. Dressed in a suit much like his, its sparse hair was matted against its skull-like visage. Greenish skin sloughed off the long bones of its arms and legs, hanging like fleshy hems at the wrists and ankles. Only one eye shimmered in the street light, the other a ragged patch of black. Its uneven, stomping gate left a trail of grave dirt from its shoes.

Catching sight of Thomas, the thing's mouth dropped open. A long, monotonous moan issued out around yellowed, broken teeth.

A staccato wave of terror and anxiety pulsed through Thomas as he looked at it. He commanded his leaden limbs to pull him up from the casket as the impulse to run from the advancing thing overcame him. Even free from the confines of the grave, he couldn't move fast enough, could barely move at all. His feet slid in the loose dirt between his shoes and the casket lining, his left arm being his only means of lifting himself after his right had failed.

Thomas whimpered in a low tone. *Oh no, oh no! Oh, Lord help me!*

He looked up at the walking corpse again as it continued to shamble toward him. *What are those things? Why are they in the Kingdom of Heaven?*

He struggled to pull himself upright, finally hoisting himself to his feet. He felt something running over his legs and looked down.

Large quantities of dirt poured out from beneath his jacket and onto his pants. Confused, he batted open the coat with his left hand.

I can see my toes, he thought, the first time the portly Thomas had been able to do so for many years.

Any excitement he might have felt rushed away as earth dumped out from a gaping hole in his abdomen, falling in a lumpy cascade to the ground.

Horrified, Thomas suddenly felt as if his chest was closing in on his organs.

Oh, God! Oh, God, no! His eyes moved back up to the creatures still moving slowly toward him. *It can't be! Can't be!*

He stumbled back, nearly falling over the edge of the grave. Stepping up and out of the pit, he lost his left shoe as something cracked in his lower legs. Thomas's mind whirled and he felt as if the world were pressing on him from all directions at once.

Much of the cemetery was undulating with movement, both above and below ground now. Corpses in various states of decay moved about the lots, walking, crawling, pulling themselves in one way or another. Some, like the first ones Thomas had seen, moved toward others. Some wandered randomly, heedless of paths or direction. A few remained motionless. All the while, more and more were digging or pushing their way up through the grass. The scraping of stone and movements of dirt mixed with scattered, wordless cries that needled into the night sky.

This isn't what we were promised! Thomas screamed in his mind. *This isn't what the preacher said it would be!*

He angled himself toward the marker for Laura's grave, next to his own. He stumbled forward and fell, tripping over his toes and landing on his hands and knees with a blurted groan.

Thomas felt the earth shifting and sliding beneath his palms, a now-familiar scrabbling winding up to his ears. The topsoil broke apart and skeletal fingers poked through. Bits of concrete, the remnants of the shattered grave vault, punctured the dirt like incisors tearing into a crust of bread. As the digits continued to tear upward, Thomas recognized the ring on the left hand instantly.

A guttural moan was all that came out of Thomas as he tried to scream. Needing to howl his sorrow and anger away he reached up to grab his throat. His clumsy hand missed the mark and slapped against the middle of his face, his fingers somehow hitting both cheekbones. They slid down his jaw and neck, meeting far less resistance than they should have. Realizing the implication, Thomas began to shake.

He pushed himself away from the grave, scooting fitfully along the ground. His voice was a ragged, lilting string of wordless bleats as he tried, over and over, to soothe the bubbling emotions in his chest through speech.

The world seemed very distant to Thomas, as if he were viewing the graveyard, the tombstones, the moving dead from somewhere deep within his own body. His senses lacked a feeling of wholeness and uniformity, like seeing through the multi-lensed eyes of an insect.

A sharp, sudden noise and a flash of even more intense light snapped Thomas back into cognizance. To his right, the clear, bright blue and red lights of a police car cut through the darkness alongside the blaring siren. The doors swept open, the windows and shiny black paint bouncing the graveyard's lights back at Thomas. An officer leapt out of each side, standing with their arms over the tops of the door, guns drawn. They were shouting, though Thomas couldn't tell to whom.

Help! he thought, rising. *Help me!*

He lurched forward, almost tumbling over again as he dragged his body in an uneven gait. He raised a hand pleadingly.

Please, officer, help me! My wife. Help! All that Thomas could force from his throat was another unintelligible moan.

This drew the nearest officer's attention. Fear in his voice, he swore, pivoted quickly on his heel, and fired.

Thomas suddenly found himself on his back, looking up into the night again. He could feel the new hole in his ribcage left by the officer's bullet. Thomas writhed on the ground, mewling. His fingers dug at the earth, pulling up grass and dirt.

The world felt bisected, a shattered mirror, each piece being looked at simultaneously. He couldn't look away. No sense in the pieces, no sense in the whole. He tried to make sense of all of it, all at once.

Another bang and Thomas lost part of his right shoulder, the arm beneath it becoming completely useless. His low cry was a remembrance of the pain he knew he should be feeling.

Rolling over, yanking himself forward, Thomas's moans continued as he crawled toward the squad car.

Kill me! Please, kill me!

He seemed to be sitting in a tiny, tiny room within his own body, curled in a frightened, useless position of hollow despair.

Another bullet cut through him. He clambered on, only a few feet from the vehicle now.

Kill me.

The officers' shouts were even louder now, heard between the barks of their handguns. The cemetery's other inhabitants were, like Thomas, marching toward the police, inexorable as an incoming tide.

Thomas's thoughts were jumbled. *You have to- This isn't- We can't- Laura! Laura! Save us! Why- forsaken us?!*

Kill me. Kill me, damn you!

Hot rage abruptly burned through the confusion in Thomas's mind, turning thought to ash. His vision blurred, tinged crimson, and he hissed inarticulately. His legs, flushed with unexpected vigor, hurled him forward like a jackrabbit.

He crashed into the police car's door, bowling the officer back, pinning him to the frame. The gun fired next to Thomas's left ear, the bullets hurtling by futilely, as the officer cried out in pain and terror.

Thomas pressed against the door, constricting the officer's lower legs and ribs. His left hand wrapped around the policeman's elbow, fingers contracting like a vice, pulling the limb over the edge of the door. The officer screamed as his flesh buckled under the pressure.

Roaring in the officer's face, venting its unearthly anger, the thing that had been Thomas Packer slowly crushed the man to death.

About the Author

Scott B. Smith

Scott is a lifelong resident of rural Northwest Georgia, near the town of Cartersville. For over 10 years, he has held a day job as a technical writer and educational designer of middle and high school curriculum. He has been a fan of science fiction and fantasy since he was quite young, primarily due to his mother (who introduced him to the genres) and '80s cartoons (which conveniently fed the addiction). He has thus far had stories published by Polar Studios and Source Point Press.

Bluebeard's Undead Brides:
A Fairy Tale Retold

By Christopher Bleakley

Sweeping west through Marche and Poitou, Angoumois and Saintonge, the great pestilence took what it could it from all that fell across its devastating path. Horses, birds, pigs and people; none were safe from its indiscriminate extirpation. Finally, insatiable in its desire to take away life and leave bloodied, blackened and pus covered corpses in its wake, the filthy bacilli reached Aunis. Following the gentle slope of the land towards the coast, the plague tore through the last of the living, transforming the fresh, salty sea air into an atmosphere filled with the stench of putrefying flesh. Finally, exhausted of victims, the virus reached the littoral sands, went beyond them in the wind, and was blown away from the memory of its ravaging journey.

However, the contagion hadn't destroyed everything. Deep in the Aunis countryside, locked up in the fortress of Charente Castle, the manic landowner Duc Pierre Perrault had sealed himself off from the horrors that raged outside. Though as wealthy as the King of France himself, Duc Pierre Perrault had never been popular with his tenants, vassals or serfs. His appearance alone brought fear into the hardest of soldiers and the blood-thirstiest of murderers. Later legends told how even the plague itself had been too afraid to enter the Duc's castle, such was his fearsome reputation and dazzling looks, for the Duc had been cursed with an enormous beard of thick blue hair that coruscated in all directions as brilliant as cobalt. Likewise, his shoulder-length locks— each strand as thick as hawser—shone as a thousand sapphires reflected in a thousand looking-glasses. Buried somewhere beneath this ferocious mane and feral facial hair was a wrinkled, leathery, yellow-colored face, in which two large eyes blazed red with hatred and blood. With a chest as large as a gorilla's and legs as thick as an elephant's the Duc's reputation as a monster among men was well founded. The locals called him *La Barbe Bleu*—Bluebeard—but never so close to him that he might hear the way they talked.

For thirteen months Bluebeard had holed himself up in his castle, drinking wine by the gallon and eating salted beef by the stone, awaiting the day the savage epidemic passed and he could go out into the world again to claim a new wife. For Bluebeard had a habit of collecting wives and had married often before. Yet, the fates of the poor women who'd fallen under his wicked spell had forever become unknown Invariably, they disappeared within weeks of their weddings. Back in the days when the living still populated the rolling plains of western France, when the land was still fertile, sprouting wondrous flora, there had been much speculation and idle chit-chat about the antics in Charente Castle once the drawbridge had been raised. But that it remained: Mere rumour and gossip.

One morning, looking out across acres of his ransacked land, all strewn with the bloated corpses of farmhands and their cattle, the weird looking Duc felt that finally his imprisonment was over. He had woken with something in his veins telling him that the dangerous disease had passed and that a new age of pleasure awaited him. His instincts proved sound. A little less than a mile away from where he stood at his chamber window, where a thick forest of oak trees marked the border of his land, a sparkle in the early day sun caught the old aristocrat's eye. He stared in deep concentration, breathing heavily, not daring to blink, as the ill-defined figure left the trees behind it and fully revealed itself. Was it naked or dressed in white? From this distance it was difficult to tell. The only surety was that it was human in form and moving slowly in a narrow zigzag, meandering this way then that, as a village drunkard after a third yard of ale. However, Bluebeard's keen eyes could see that this was no drunkard. He squinted to enhance his vision.

"By the dogs!" he murmured to himself, his voice gruff and hoarse from fourteen moons of rest. "C'est une jeune fille! A maiden, or I'll be damned. Le pauvre lapin! Mon Dieu! I must have her at once."

Without another thought the Duc threw off his night dress, threw on his best doublet and breeches, and raced from his sleeping quarters down the spiral steps that led to the castle vestibule. There, using all the strength his massive arms possessed, he pulled upon a wooden lever set at the side of two large iron doors. The lever released a mechanism—the doors swung open and the drawbridge outside lowered itself across the moat. Still unthinking, Bluebeard ran across the platform as fast as his rotund frame could manage, for the plague had taken all his horses a whole year before, leaving them to rot in the stables in the castle's south wing. Once across the moat he stopped, out of breath, but never once did his eye wander from the mesmerising figure as it approached him on its oscillating path. Bluebeard started closer.

"Salut!" he cried, flapping his chubby arms high in the air. "Ici! Je suis ici!"

The figure stopped momentarily, and gazed blankly through opaque eyes at the origin of the call, but never once looked directly at the Duc. Bluebeard felt a sudden, unnerving connection, but shrugged it off as a change in the breeze. Without further fuss, the figure started towards the excited aristocrat. In turn, Bluebeard moved towards it, a semblance of pity in his eye, an eruption of malignence in his heart. Finally, the two strangers were close enough to speak in ordinary tones. Bluebeard stared inquisitively at the girl. Her face was vacant, grey and gaunt, her green eyes pale and her long blonde hair greasy and soiled, but the Duc thought there was something familiar about her countenance. She wore a much torn, full length cotton night dress—which although dirty with mud and stains had clearly been made by a gifted seamstress —which Bluebeard also thought he'd seen before. The girl's feet were bare, encrusted with muck. Yet, through this unappetizing, oddly congruous exterior, Bluebeard could see—he knew—that she had once been (and with a bit of meat and drink would again be) a true and wholesome beauty. Her charisma-free aura and clumsy and awkward manner would soon be rectified. Bluebeard had had many women, and every one of them had succumbed to him in the end.

"Oh! My poor darling," said Bluebeard, a mock empathy in his tone. "What horrors have you seen? Come, malheureux enfant, we'll soon have you right."

Smiling a crooked smile through his cerulean whiskers the aristocrat took the young girl by the arm. He recoiled suddenly as he felt the terrifying coldness of her skin, even though the day was cloudless and the sun shone with the warmth of a thick woollen blanket. He took her soft hand and rubbed it between his own, but the chill remained.

"By the dogs! Come, child, you are frozen. Let us get you inside. I have food and fire, hot water and clean clothes. Soon you will have your strength."

As he spoke, Bluebeard's mind crammed itself with thoughts of his future with this fey beauty; strange thoughts of a future that was also a memory. His mind raced ahead involuntarily. Already, he was considering where to locate a priest, so that he could marry his new-found nubile without further ado. *"Surely somebody at the monastery survived,"* he brooded. *"Those monks are as tough as trees, by the dogs!"* The girl appeared to have read Bluebeard's thoughts, and though she looked at her suitor through dispassionate eyes, the subtle smile spreading across her face told the Duc everything he wanted to know. Gripping the girl firmly, he escorted her back across the fields.

They reached the castle and Bluebeard provided for the girl, but she refused both food and drink, and rejected all attempts at conversation. All she took from her host was a black evening gown which had belonged to one of his erstwhile wives. Bluebeard had never known a woman to defy him so and as twilight came he demanded an explanation.

"No more softly, softly, ma chérie," he said, grimacing. "I rescue you from wandering, bring you into my home, clothe you, and offer you food and drink, which you impertinently ignore. It is enough, by the dogs! I have had my fill of this discourteous behavior. I cannot stand this in a future wife."

For the first time, the girl spoke and Bluebeard was taken aback. "A future wife?"

Her voice was faint and distant, yet resounded clearly through the grand space of the castle's dining room. She continued, pausing substantially between the words. "I…am…to…be…your… future…wife?"

"Of course you are! Why, by the dogs, do you think you are here? Out of the goodness of my heart?"

A peculiar look appeared across the young girl's face, one that showed she acknowledged the irony of Bluebeard's last words.

"The goodness of your heart," she repeated, enigmatically.

"I'll show you the goodness of my heart!" he shrieked. "I will leave now, by the dogs, and head to the monastery. There I will engage a priest to return with me here. Upon the morning we shall be wed. Make no mistake about that, by the dogs!"

As he finished speaking he threw his head back, let out a tremendous roar of laughter that combined both the cackle of a deranged warlock and the guffaw of a duplicitous nobleman, and stood clapping his hands like a manic marionette. The young girl remained unmoved as she sat at the dining table, but imperceptibly the corners of her mouth turned down. For an instant the dullness in her green eyes flashed turquoise, but Bluebeard didn't see. Once he'd finished his performance and calmed down, he pulled a large gold ring from his belt, on which hung a dozen and a half gold keys of varying sizes.

"Now, ma chérie, before I go, here are the keys to every room in the castle. You are free to roam, to look around, to enter any room you choose."

Bluebeard paused, narrowed his eyes, then took the largest key between his fat finger and thumb. He held it up vertically so that all the other keys fell loose on the ring beneath. There was great theatre in his movements.

"But this key, mon pauvre lapin, you do not use. By the dogs! You do not use this key. The door which this key opens is forbidden to you. The room beyond that door is forbidden to you. You must not use this key, open the door, or enter the room."

The aristocrat moved close to the young girl as he spoke, then pressed his ugly flaxen face right up to hers, spittle flying from his mouth as he repeated his warning, splashing across her cold cheeks like the slaver of a rabid hound. His eyes flared with lunacy. Trapped in her chair the girl said nothing, felt nothing, did nothing.

"Comprenez-tu?"

The girl smiled serenely. She understood.

"Good. Now, nightfall is upon us and I have no horse, by the dogs! This wretched plague. This wretched plague! I will have to walk to the monastery, ma chérie and there I will spend the night amongst the monks. I will return with the priest before the sun has fully risen. The castle is yours, my precious one, but do not—Do not! by the dogs, do not!—enter the room of which I have spoken. Jusqu'à demain, ma chérie!" Bluebeard left the castle and went out into the dark moonless night.

The girl picked up the keys from where they'd been left on the table, and toyed with them idly in both hands. She had no interest in the castle or its many rooms. Except for one. *That* room. She did not care for the room through the curiosity so often found in carefree youth, or from the rebellious nature that juveniles thrive on annoying their elders with. Nothing could have been further from the truth. The reality for this girl was that she had once, not so very long ago, been an inhabitant of this castle and *that* room, along with many others who had suffered Bluebeard's relentless cruelty. In *that* room lay the forgotten corpses of Bluebeard's many wives.

Knowing exactly where to go the girl got up from the table and left the dining room. She proceeded at a heavy pace down a draughty corridor until she reached a door that opened onto a flight of stone steps that descended into blackness. She lit a torch from a sconce burning nearby, and with its light as her guide, tentatively made her way down to the cellar. Rats scurried across her still unshod feet, suddenly disturbed by the luminescence, but the girl was not afraid. Nor was she unable to stomach the stench of feces and decay, of rot and consumption that invaded her nostrils and would have made any living soul retch. However, this girl was no living soul. All the life-force had been taken from her a long time ago, at Bluebeard's heinous hand and all that had been left of her was an atrophying cadaver. She was just one. Others too, many many others, had succumbed to Bluebeard's brutal madness.

The girl splashed through the fetid water that covered the cobbled basement floor, the fire of the orange torch aiding her vision. Finally, she came to the portal she was searching for. She took the gold key, slid it into the lock, and turned it a half-circle counter-clockwise. Gently she pushed the door. It opened inward with ease.

Stepping inside, the girl was met with the most revolting sight. In the light of the flickering flame could be seen a cell whose floor and walls and ceiling were painted with blood, the blood of so many unfortunate brides. Around the walls, some on hooks, some in nooses, the bodies of Bluebeard's victims hung, all lifeless and drooping free. The girl was not afraid, for here she was in the company of her most intimate friends: Eleanor, Maria, and Josephine; Anne, Sophia and Caroline; other ex-Duchesses and more mistresses besides, all of whom had vanished upon wedlock with the murderous Duc.

In an ordered, deliberate manner, the young girl moved steadily around the room and bit the little finger on the left hand of every corpse. Within an instant, each lifeless mass became animated, as the spirit of the undead passed into them. Low moans and groans soon filled the room as the dead were painfully resurrected. Loosening the nooses from around their necks, lifting themselves from off the meat-hooks they'd been strung up on, the newly dynamic ones had a strength that only awaited the right challenge to display itself.

As the night passed, the assembly was added to. Dishevelled, some with creased skin, others with their flesh pulled taut across their bony frames, the former wives and lovers congregated one by one on the underground chamber's bloodied floor. Sophia, with her long brown locks now matted in clumps; Caroline, her flame-red curls now a mass of moss; Maria, her blonde pigtails now the colour and texture of straw. Josephine's once brilliant blue eyes now charcoal grey; Anne's once rosy cheeks now the colour of slate. All knew what had happened to them and why the young girl had come.

Slowly, the procession of unarticulated mannequins moved back along the dark, underground corridor to ascend the granite staircase. In single file they traipsed into the dining room, each taking a seat at the grand table. Soon, no free space was left, as the wives of Bluebeard—once dead, killed by the aristocrat's own foul will, now undead, brought back to the sentient world through the terrible gift bestowed on one of their sorority—waited for their nemesis to return.

The sun rose on that dreadful day as Bluebeard came back to Charente Castle. He was in a sore-headed mood—not unusually for him—as he'd been told at the monastery that no one was available to perform the Blessed Sacrament. Another month, the monks had said, before a priest would be able to make the trip from the neighboring county town.

"By the dogs!" he yelled as he entered the castle. "What use are these inane religious folk? I am Duc Pierre Perrault! I own everything I see! And a man cannot be wed without the presence of one of these blathering buffoons? Ma chérie, where are you?"

"In here."

The voice came from the dining room, though to Bluebeard it sounded like the voice of a dozen. The sound had a strange layered texture to it, as that of a chorus in a large and empty church.

Bluebeard turned toward the dining room door, opened it and entered.

He did not take another step forward. Every muscle in him seized; every bone became as unflinching as a broadsword.

Before him stood an array of mad, vengeful and determined creatures. All at once, they were beautiful and ugly, affable and repellent. A cast of the damned, all pale faces, moulting hair, melting flesh, crooked teeth, the remains of Bluebeard's former spouses. He opened his mouth, but the very air in his lungs had become immobile. The aristocrat remained fixed to the spot, paralysed with the intense fear that only one who comes face to face with their own impending doom can ever understand.

"By—"

A faint exhalation, but nothing more.

The young girl spoke. "Your time is over, Duc Bluebeard!"

"Hissssssss!" came the shocking approval of the other ghouls, as the sound of a thousand Medusas. "Hissssssss!"

"I swore I would avenge myself, and all those who were lost before me."

"Hissssssss!"

"I was the last to put your accursed ring on my finger; the last to suffer the torture of your diabolical brain."

"Hissssssss!"

"But the plague revived me and now I have revived all the others."

A thought flashed through Bluebeard's mind. It couldn't be. It was! He knew he had recognised her from the first instant. Yes! It was her, Antonia, the woodcutter's daughter and the last of his duchesses.

"I was dead, and no pestilence, however terrible, can kill the dead. But by the dogs—Ha-ha-ha-ha-ha! What a silly, silly phrase you have—where that vile virus took away the breath of the living, it breathed new life into the already dead. And now we are back in unison to exact our dues."

Bluebeard summoned all his strength to throw up his arms in defence, to lash out, or to flee; but his energy was deployed in vain. Within seconds the host of gruesome women was upon

139

Bluebeard's terrified person, scratching blood from his flesh, tearing hair from his beard and scalp with jagged black incisors, gouging at his eyes with brown fingernails, feeding off his wantonness until nothing remained but a congealed shapeless bulk of skin, bone and blue hair turned purple with torrents of blood.

Their appetites satiated, Bluebeard's undead brides fell exhausted to the floor.

END

About the Author

Christopher Bleakley

Christopher Bleakley is a lawyer currently working in Prague, Czech Republic. Suffering legal nightmares during the day he likes to relax with literary nightmares in the evenings. A fan of horror and other weird fiction since childhood, particularly the classic English ghost story, he has been writing short stories in various genres for the last few years, but not nearly as many as he would like to. He is currently working on his first collection.

His publishing credits include: spinetinglers.co.uk; stories in the Static Movement anthologies *Cobwebs and Antiquities* and *Medieval Nightmares*; a story in the Crooked Cat charity anthology *Fear*; a story in the *Were-Traveler* ezine; a story in the recently published ebook *Things We Can Create* (Stone Thread Publishing); a science fiction story on www.short-story.me; and an article which will appear later in the year in the zombie themed Z Magazine.

Pale Brother

By Zach Chapman

My brother's dead. Not undead. He's dead dead. I know I'm not the first to lose a brother, but I feel a compulsion to write down his story. Our story. They say that writing about something won't bring it back, but that isn't necessarily true. George'll live a little longer in my mind and he'll live how he used to be. The way he was before the bite. Before he came back from war. George will live again with that crooked smile so similar to the one I used to see in my mirror, just like he was when we traded every bat, bullet and scratched penny we had for that car.

We were the first and probably the only folks in the Huntington Shelter to own a Challenger, or any car that wasn't a rusty piece of shit, at least since the biters started chewing up the scenery. I know what you are thinking: How the hell does some country punk earn enough scratch to pay for a ride, a late twenty teens Dodge Challenger, if I may boast? Maybe you're even thinking: How the hell does a young punk even survive outside the cities? We were hard. We knew how to play the game just right. It wasn't just evident to us. Folks could see it in our eyes. They could see it in our scars and broken noses. They could see it in our chipped and missing teeth. We weren't just brutes, George and I had wits. We could even read a little.

At ten I had conned my way into several petty jobs in the neighboring shelters. Burning bodies, building perimeters, that sort of thing. A year later I was bringing Georgie out scouting. By the time I was thirteen, Georgie and I were selling fake holy water on the side of the road to anyone but the locals. My sign said, "Saves your life in a pinch with just a pinch of holy water. 25 cents." I wonder how many morons got chewed once they found out our water weren't so holy.

It wasn't long before Georgie and I were splatting zombies for scratch. At first the scratch was pretty bad, but eventually our name got around to the neighboring shelters, Bennington, Nassau,

Fairfield and even New Haven, Connecticut. If you had a problem, we had a solution. If your dearly departed wasn't so dearly departed we had an axe, a gun, a bullet, a bat, a chainsaw. You know the drill, no pun intended, you've had to deal with one at some point in your life, aim for the head, or a heavy blow to the skull will do the trick.

Our cells were ringing not stop. We had to start subcontracting which soon led to people working under us. Before we were twenty, we owned a business and business was slashing, smashing and above all, booming. We only lost a few and only at first, none of the good ones. Georgie used to say, "If you're good, ya don't get bit. Ya don't even get close."

So, we employed a few talented people and the rest was history. I had an empire, of sorts, and scratch, lots of scratch. Girls too. The finest birds you'd see in New England outside the cities. Georgie had a new one every week. Before we lost it all, all of my employees shipped off to the Border Wars or went to the loony bin, all 'cept me-- I'll get to the particulars of that later, I was in Bennington with Georgie having fresh fish and chips with a heavy splash of vinegar for dinner at the only diner in the shelter. We had just finished a particularly messy job. Blood flecked our work clothes like oil on a mechanic. From where we sat, we saw that Challenger just on the outside of Bennington's chain link barrier with a trade sign in the window begging us to take a closer look. We both wolfed down our fish.

Our shit rusted Honda Civic was always parked in view. We had too many supplies in there to risk otherwise. Georgie pulled it up next to the Challenger, and we waited for its owner. Right before dusk a fat little man waddled out from the shanty shadows of Bennington towards the Dodge. What was left of the man's hair was sad and he constantly slicked his palm over it while he spoke.

"You boys can't afford a runner like this," when he spoke the fat of his chin jiggled. I remember wondering why this guy hadn't become food for the chewers and how the hell he could have been so fat. I decided rather quickly it must have had something to do with the car.

"You're interested in a trade though, right?" Georgie asked.

"Yes. But I'm not looking for a Honda. Rust like that is littered all over the old highways. I'm looking for supplies. A lot of supplies. Food. Seeds. Guns. Ammo. Penicillin. Tobacco. Good clothing. Maybe some vintage wine? Food for a city." He chuckled nervously, no doubt wondering if we'd kill him and just take the Challenger.

"The Honda is full of supplies. Take a look." Georgie said.

That was an understatement. The entire back was bulging full of weapons and ammo that we'd stockpiled from contracts. My two Sigs, Georgie's Kimbers, still gleaming with gun oil. We even had a box full of oxycodone. Not to mention two shoe-boxes full of quarters and dimes. Back then a dime could buy you more than just a coke. However, all our supplies wasn't half of a peak runner's worth. Good runners were hard to come by and this Challenger looked peak. With a car like that, out-racing gangs and chew herds became possible. We could leave New England if we wanted.

The fat man chuckled at Georgie. "I'm looking for more supplies than that. I am gathering for Wertheim. They've got a lot of mouths to feed, boy."

Being called 'boy' irritated Georgie. I could tell. His mouth twitched just like mine. They argued back and forth for maybe five minutes and I could tell this squat fat man wasn't going to budge, but Georgie was mad. He wouldn't let it go.

I blame his anger and my infatuation with their argument for not hearing the rustle in the pines behind the little man. The biter must have heard the argument. Coming right out from the trees, he went straight for the fat man's neck. His panic was almost satisfying to see. Panic quickly turned to terror as they both tumbled to the ground. The man smashed his bald head on a rock. Georgie was quick to pry the biter off the owner of the Challenger and I crushed its skull with the bottom of my grubby boot heels.

144

We made sure he wasn't bit, and he wasn't, but the man was out cold.

Georgie told me the stranger owed us his life and that the Challenger would be sufficient payment. I shrugged. I didn't need much convincing. We stuffed him in our old Honda, relieved him of his keys, then made our way back to Huntington in our new Challenger.

I can't blame the demise of our splattering business on the Border War, not really. George and I took off that winter. We left Jimmy in charge. We shouldn't have left Jimmy in charge, but this isn't about the business, that's another story entirely, maybe another ten.

We left New England, nothing over our shoulders but a foggy iced rear window attached to the slickest runner you ever saw. She had two light grey stripes down her polished black back. You can imagine the sight we made against the bright white snow. Beautiful. Yes, we turned quite a few heads.

George and I drove to Texas. Why not? On the highways that were clear, we could really get her going. We topped her out at 175 on I40 just after a pit stop outside Nashville; I had to yell at the top of my lungs to get George to slow the hell down. It was too damn dangerous to do that with the cold roads, an ice patch could have ended our vacation early.

It took us four days to get to Austin. Pretty good time right? Well, we did hit up one brothel and a couple bars. Texas culture was so different from New England's. We could have never run a business there! There were so many guns. I only recall seeing a few chewers during our brief stay in Austin and everyone had each other's backs. Naturally, they were wary of outsiders, but after a few days they warmed up to us. I told Georgie I wanted to go south and see The Alamo. He looked at me confused.

"The Alamo, Georgie! You don't remember The Alamo? There's some legend about it. It's like where the Texans made their last stand. Three hundred of them fought off the entire Mexican Army and won the war."

I was sitting at a bar when I said this. Drunk on Sixth Street, or Fifth. I can't remember. I must have barked it a little too loud. The bartender poured me another glass of light yellow pissfire while making and not breaking an awkward eye contact.

"It didn't happen like that."

I knew this man was just going to tell me the legends weren't true. I wasn't going to have it. Before he could get another thought, out I downed the drink, shoved off, stiffed on the tip and grabbed George by his muscular shoulder.

So, a day later, we headed south. Austin had been nice enough, the people, the sights, the cheery good moods of the population, so the bleak change in scenery was a hard bite to swallow. In between the hill country, on the long stretches of highway, we saw dozens of bloated chewers. These ones weren't like the ones back home. These chewers were fatter. Hungrier, if that's possible and there were so many of them.

It was about an hour south of Austin when we saw her. She was a small stick fleeing a mass of chewers along the side of the I35. Georgie had me to thank for her. If it wasn't for me, they'd never have met.

"Pull over!" he said.

"What?" My response was haughty. We'd seen people pulled apart, chewed, gutted, nipped, bit — whatever you want to call it, once a month, sometimes more.

"You want us to pull over? Risk getting chew blood all over the hood?"

"It's black. It's not that big of a deal and we hit three since Nashville, you didn't say anything then."

"You're jumping out. If you get bit, I'm not blowing your brains out and I won't let you do it either. Waste of a damn bullet." We joked. He smiled.

We picked her up. No one got bit. No real surprise there. George was talented. Then, we headed back north, because south towards The Alamo was too risky — too many herds. We drove until we hit Waco, where we stopped for drinks and conversation with our new acquaintance who had said little on the ride there. I imagine she might have been wondering if her escape from the chewers was just another hell altogether, with my brother and I carrying the pitchforks. We didn't always look like the most pleasant folk.

As I got out of the car, I fully noticed what this woman looked like. She was gorgeous. Stunning. How could I have missed it before? And for half the day! My god! My brother was right for demanding us to stop. She was the most attractive woman I'd ever seen. She looked like a city woman, not anything like what George and I was used to. I am not a monogamous man, but after seeing this beauty — her name, I didn't even know it yet— I could respect a man for choosing the path. Her hair was a rich dark chocolate, it fell only to her shoulders and even there it wasn't cut straight, but the style seemed on purpose. Her eyes were five colors at once. Brown, green, blue, yellow and I swear there was a bit of red in there too. Her nose had a silver ring in it, and so did her eyebrow.

George stared at her ass as he held open the pub door. It was roomy. This time we didn't sit at the bar, but a red window side booth. George was having trouble not looking at her endowment as she spoke.

"Where are you boys heading?"

"Back home." I said

"Where's home?"

"New England." George said. "Where's yours?"

"Don't know yet. You have a nice car."

"Thanks."

The conversation fumbled about awkwardly at first, then rolled through the normal topics of introductions and explanations. After that, we hit it off. Over our mud colored drinks she laughed at our stories and asked for more. We told jokes, horror stories and even heard a few from her, until it was far after sunset and last call. We stumbled out of the bar like old friends, George pushing me playfully, Autumn — that was her name — following closely behind.

We didn't head straight home. Cut up through Oklahoma and Missouri. We poked about the safer spots, the small towns with thick fences. Tons of chewers ambled on the back roads, but there wasn't as much snow as you'd think. The thing about snow is it slows down the biters, but it can put you in a bind too, give it too much gas, you slide out of control, same goes for the brakes. So, after seeing a few herds, we stuck to the highways.

After the fifth night, George was sleeping with Autumn. Depending on where we were staying, how thick the walls were, or if it was a hostile, I could hear them. I have to admit, I was jealous. If I ever let it show, they never made any mention of it. I saw their relationship blossom and aside from the gnawing jealous twang eating my guts at night, I was happy for them. I truly was. In a world so full of death, so much that it's literally overflowing, it's nice to see two so in love. Georgie looked at her with something other than lust in his hazel eyes. It was something so foreign to me to see in him.

They couldn't wait for Huntington. They got married in a church in New Jersey. Maybe that's what cursed them? Obviously, I was the best man. The ceremony couldn't have lasted more than fifteen minutes, but it was nice enough. The priest was of the Irish variety. His voice was as powerful as it was funny. We drank away half the night in Jersey and when they retired I stayed out, walking the streets.

When we came back to Huntington, I was devastated. The business was dead. George had Autumn at least, but I was left with the dregs of a business to lament on. I tried for the better part of a year to start it back up, but people didn't trust the name anymore. I didn't have enough money to recruit people and not enough jobs to even need recruitment. Two other splatter firms popped up in our absence and they stole most of the clientele. Georgie and I were forced to do cheap-paying supply runs with the Challenger.

In July, a recruiter came by the duplex we were renting. George and Autumn lived on the tidy side of the structure separated by me and my mess by a thin particle board membrane. The recruiter must have been making his rounds in the New York wastelands going door-to-door warmongering. He shook hands with George and I. I didn't care for his wet fingers and clammy palms. I caught onto his bullshit, but he disillusioned Georgie about the Border War. He said it would be safer than strolling a baby through the park, and that the service paid handsomely. Maybe my brother was thinking of saving up for a future kid or maybe he was just tired of living off nothing. Either way, two weeks later he went to war. Autumn cried. I tried to talk him out of it, but away he went.

Six months passed. I heard horrible stories about the Border Wars. A client told me that they ordered soldiers to shoot biters and humans alike, anyone coming near our border got a bullet in the head. I had trouble imagining little Georgie killing real people.

One day Autumn ran into my side of the duplex without knocking. The slanted stacks of my dirty dishes piled in the kitchen sink and slight unchanged feline litter aroma suddenly ashamed me, though she seemed to take no notice. She was holding a yellow letter. Weeping.

I knew what the yellow letter meant, or could mean. We sat down on the couch huddled together. It was the closest I'd ever been and would ever be to Autumn. In a way, I never wanted it to end. In a way, I hated it. Together we opened the yellow letter. I felt the air escape her lungs under my arm. George had been injured, but not to worry, he'd make a full recovery. They treated the wound soon enough. I could feel relief fill her, but I wasn't so sure.

A month later George came home. He was holding a box of all the money he'd earned fighting to secure our borders and a small folded note. My first reaction to my brother coming home? A handshake? A slap on the back? A hug? A bear hug? None of these. Revulsion. His slow gate was all too familiar. His shoes shuffled against the concrete. His jaw was slack and when I saw his eyes, they were dull and had little life in them. My heart sank. From somewhere distant behind me, I heard Autumn make an inarticulate moan.

We ate dinner that night on George and Autumn's side of the duplex. She had roasted a turkey that morning and prepared a delicious meal. I couldn't even taste it. We ate in silence. I couldn't keep my eyes off of George. I located the bite; it was his right ear. In its wake only a black wilted piece of meat and cartilage remained. Seeing it made me stop eating my tasteless dinner. Autumn tried to make conversation. Bless her; even in her agony she looked so damn beautiful, "What's that you got there, honey?"

She gently opened his pale palm. Easily enough he gave up the folded note. It read: "We are glad to have administered one of the first ever zombification recovery treatments to this applicant. Given time, the subject is to make a full recovery. Thank you for this opportunity and for the subject's service." Then as a footnote, "The medical care charge has been already been deducted from subject's income and at this time is nonrefundable."

George stared at his food for a while, as if trying to figure out what it was. By the end of dinner he had chewed on some pink turkey meat until it drooled out of his mouth and rolled down his chest.

Weeks passed and no real noticeable recovery was made, aside from the obvious fact that he wasn't trying to eat us. He'd groan out half words or point at things, but the worst was his staring. He would stare at things as if he were fighting to remember. There was enough of his soul in there to make it harder on us. He would sit on my hardwood chair for hours watching the TV on my side of the duplex, their side didn't have one. At times I think he would watch it and at other times I think he was just staring off. He would sit in his chair and grip the arm rests so hard that I thought his bones would penetrate through his grey flesh and scratch against the wood. He would gnarl and gnash his teeth. At night he couldn't sleep, which meant Autumn couldn't sleep.

One night when George was on the other side of the house, I threw the remote through the TV. Later that night, Autumn came over. She was crying. She cried a lot back then, the reason was obvious. She confessed that she thought he'd never be the same. I didn't know what to do. I just watched her there, sitting and sniffling on the couch. I tried to reassure her. "But the letter," I said. The letter had said he would. She shook her head and after a long grim silence Autumn reached for my hand. I drew back slightly.

"Lewis," she said. "Love me."

What was the look she gave me? Hopeful? Lustful? Hurt? Desperate? Love? All except that last one. I was shocked and as much as I wanted to take her hand and kiss her chapped lips, red eyes and pale cheeks, she was my brother's wife. I did not betray him and so she sulked to her side of the duplex. Whenever I saw her the next few nights she would look at me with longing, not caring whether George saw her courts. Each time I timidly refused, though I regret that now.

That was a few days before I heard the scratching. It was on her side of the duplex in their bathroom. The sound had been nagging me for hours so I decided to see what was going on. George was sitting in a chair at the dinner table deaf to the horrible noise. I strolled past him and he didn't stutter. The door was locked and the rat or whatever was scratching on the other side wouldn't let me in. I used a paperclip to fumble the privacy lock open.

Autumn was in there, but it wasn't exactly Autumn. She was dead and had turned. Her beautiful face was a twisted grey snarl. My first instinct was that George had bit her. I yelled his name in anger, but then I saw the rope around her neck and the blood soaking into the bath mat. Her wrists were a mangled mess of flesh, tendons and veins, her wounds self-inflicted. The rope around her neck kept her from getting to me and she would have; I was immobilized. Terror. Shock. Indescribable sadness. Had this not been my fault? If I had just held her more, if I had just kissed her, if I had, George forgive me, just taken her to bed, would this have happened? Why did she not put a bullet in her brain? Why did she have to let herself come back? Was this some kind of poetic irony she plagued on me? I often have those are thoughts now.

As she crawled forward, fighting the thin rope, George, having heard his name, had finally come over. He shrieked. The voice was not biter, not human. He shoved me to the ground and tried to hold her. This vivid image haunts my brain: Her arms out stretched for me, her mouth open, as she fought against her husband's tight, somehow loving, embrace and fixed her undead eyes right at mine.

Moments later, I blew out her brains. That was the first night I really saw something human on George's face since he came back from service.

And so begun the bachelor life all over again. I kid only because I need to. I often sat staring at George thinking of taking him to an institution. Give him back to the government, right? Maybe they could use him? However, I couldn't do that. He was my brother for Christ's sake. I moved us out of the duplex and into a small two-room shanty. I took him out for rides in the Challenger once a night and we took shifts walking the perimeter of Huntington. The color in his face seemed to gradually turn from grey to pale. At first I thought it was just my imagination, but after he started mumbling halfhearted sentences I knew something inside him was changing. I started letting him shoot some of the chewers while we walked our patrols. It served two purposes. It put the townsfolk to ease about George walking around and it made George happy. Sliver by sliver the old George started showing itself. Instead of not eating anything at all, he'd eat a nibble of raw steak every few nights. The whites of his eyes weren't so damn grey anymore and while I witnessed this transformation of George, I wondered if it was the tragedy that triggered his transformation. Is having a broken heart the first sign of having a heart?

Half a year later, George expressed interest in going to the Susquehanna River for a hike. By this time of year, the ice had completely melted away and green stems with bright yellow flowers grew in its place. It felt like life was returning, in more ways than one, and I could see on George's face (all except for that large black gnarl of skin that was once his ear) he felt the same. We hiked until the sunset, by George's lead and sluggish pace. My veins were pumping acid through my legs by then; I am guessing George didn't feel the same way. We found a nice delta that surrounded us by the sound of rushing water where we made a cozy fire.

In the warmth of the fire, I tried to feel like George. What thoughts went through him? What thoughts lingered? He was there but he wasn't. I tried to think like him. The practice unraveled my brain, but I was pleasant anyways, "George. I'm glad you woke up."

His face was hard, cold and white for a long time. He said nothing. Then, he did something I never guessed he could have. He cried. Silver tears raced down the wells he had for eye sockets, "Autumn." He croaked, "We'd be better off if I'd not come back from the war."

"No. No George. That's not true." I said. It would be a lie if I didn't say I thought hard about it and of the image of Autumn reaching out for me with that rope around her neck, but this time George was a man, not a monster, and he was stroking her dead black hair.

"Autumn died because of me."

"George." My inability to deal with emotions surfaced again. It was all I could say.

"She slit her wrists because of me and she fucked you."

"What?" I was taken off guard.

"She slit her wrists. She fucked you. It was my fault," his voice was grey.

"George. Autumn and I would never. Didn't ever…"

"I saw the looks. She gave you looks."

"No George. There weren't looks."

"Liar." He grabbed and shoved me. I could smell his breath: raw, rotting meat sitting in a half-decayed stomach.

"I didn't."

"Bastard," he said.

"I didn't fuck her. Maybe if I had she wouldn't have killed herself. You were a fucking chew." I immediately felt sorry, but emotions that had been crawling a narrow crooked line since Autumn's death finally manifested in my hateful words.

Slow but hard, he struck me in the jaw. His fingers found my collar. He ripped it and I push him in the chest. It felt hollow, like a dead tree. He slammed me with his cold knuckles in my gut. The wind left me as I staggered back several feet, almost losing my footing on the slick, green grass. Rearing back, I charged and tackled him to the ground. My momentum sent us rolling over to the embankment. We hadn't fought like this since before we had enough facial hair to call a beard. What was this? Had he instigated this just for a fight? Was this his idea of a good time? Then, I saw the tears again, but he was laughing, "Ha ha! Did you take good care of her?"

"Alright," I said. So this was a game, or so I thought. "I took care of her when I drove you two halfway around the goddamn world."

I longed deep down to know he knew I hadn't slept with Autumn. I couldn't help it. I was laughing. Were we kids? Was this some squabble for a girl? Was this an arm wrestling match to see who was stronger? Or maybe a foot race? He was on top of me and he was laughing too. His laugh sounded like a choking wheeze. I loved it. I hated it. I looked into his eyes, "How about we head back, shoot some chewers on the way?"

I know now it may have been the wrong thing to say. He stared off, still on top of me; his dark eyes reminded me of the hard wood chair I owned and my old TV, a remote protruding from its cracked glass. The fact I realized then was this: George was broken. No drug, no counseling, no amount of fresh air or brotherly fights could melt those shards back together. The only person who could was dead. A sound of snapping twigs on the other side of the river soiled my revelation. Someone was there. Someone was watching flashing light.

I heard a gruff voice shout, "Sir! Do you need help?"

George looked up. A way out. A new hope. Something else finally. A cure, a fucking cure. Not this bullshit half-ass "treatment" Uncle Sam cooked up. Something real. Something permanent. That's what he saw. He looked down at me.

"Hey! That man is being attacked!"

Sounds of splashes and footsteps trampled into my ears. Deep in those wells, I saw him wink. I saw his blue lips twitch a smile.

"Kill that chewer. He's attacking someone! I don't think that man has been bit yet."

"No! No!" I shrieked. I fought it as hard as I could. George had no problem pinning me down. Opening his mouth wide, George slowly brought his head near my shoulder. His breath hot, he paused for a moment. Then.Bang!

In death he looked out for me. Making sure if the shot were a near miss it would just likely penetrate my shoulder. It wasn't. It hit George right in the middle of the forehead. His brains hit a tree behind us. I felt his body go limp in my arms. By the time I rolled him off of me, my saviors, rather, his saviors, had vanished. I rolled his body into the river and watched as it, missing half a head, floated down the current. I hiked back to the car, the grass and flowers seeming more brown and grey than when the sun was out. I started the Challenger and flicked the high beams on. When had it gotten so cold? I floored it into the night. I was crying. The lights flickered then shorted out and I was alone.

About the Author

Zach Chapman

Zach was inspired to write Pale Brother from a memory of an uncle whose funeral he recently attended. He considers "Pale Brother" is the marriage of Tim O'Brien and George Romero. Zach's publication history includes; Quirk 2010 which featured "The Cell Membrane," and Quirk 2011 which published "Thirst." He has a Bachelor's in English and works as a Copy Editor by day.

The Beginning

By Leah Rhyne

Sid lounges on the tattered couch in the small living space of her mother's trailer, eating Lucky Charms and watching Saturday morning cartoons. She loves the classics – Batman, Thundercats, Transformers. She loses herself in dreams of superheroes who swoop in and rescue her, because even at nine, she knows there's a better life out there than trailer parks and Lucky Charms.

The first scream she hears confuses her.

She reaches for the remote. The sound *could* be coming from the television, but the current scene is a quiet one.

She presses mute, but the scream continues.

"Mama?" she calls, her voice tentative. She's not sure what time her mother came home last night, or even *if* she came home last night, but she tries again.

"Mama?"

"Sydney! Sid!" Her mother bursts through the flimsy bedroom door, which closes behind her with a pitiful slap. "Sid, what's going on? Are you okay?"

She looks rough: red lipstick smeared across her cheek, hair disheveled, the cotton of her t-shirt so thin it's near-transparent, stinking of sweat and old dollar bills.

She must've just gotten in, Sid thinks for a fleeting moment, flinching from the sight of her mother's nipples. Then, the scream outside is joined by more panicked voices, and Sid's gaze shifts to the front door. A hand, bloodied and clenched in an arthritic claw, slaps the window. Sid's mother screams, but Sid watches. She waits. She feels like she's still watching a show, poised on the edge of her seat.

The cheap window glass shatters. Sid's mother screams again and blocks the quaking front door with the weight of her slight body.

She looks at Sid, frozen by the couch. "Sid! Run! Find help! I don't know what's happening!"

Why can't I move?

Sid's legs are paralyzed.

Timmy, the ancient, gnarled tomcat, hisses from beneath the coffee table.

Sid's mother is knocked to the ground as the door pushes in. "Sydney Elizabeth, *go!*"

There's a back door to the trailer and Sid darts in that direction. She passes the kitchen, where the small refrigerator is hidden by Sid's drawings and papers. A puppy. A two-story house with a fence and a swing. A math test with a big, red A+. The rest of the trailer is a blur.

A burning candle falls to the ground in Sid's wake, igniting the polyester fibers of the carpet. Timmy hisses again.

Sid bursts through the back door, running as fast as her legs will carry her. Something, possibly Timmy, catches Sid's leg. She feels the burn of torn skin, the trickle of blood on her calf, but she jerks it free and runs on. She senses rather than sees the chaos around her. People running this way and that. Shouts, screams, gunfire. It's as if one of her shows has come to life, but now that it's real she doesn't want to see it. She keeps her head down and runs.

****

Mama said to find help.

That's what Sid is doing as she trips through the wildflower-speckled meadow toward the old country road. Sharp rocks dig into her bare feet, but they're the least of her concerns.

When she looks over her shoulder, she sees smoke that rises, thick and greasy, over the trailer park. The fire's grown quickly and she wonders if its catalyst was the small candle from her own trailer.

158

Sid, breathless and frightened, has stopped running. Instead she walks, slowly, carefully, seeking help.

Sid has no idea where help is, but she knows it's not back at the trailer park, which belches flames like an angry dragon.

Not that there was ever any help at the trailer park. Not for Sid. Not for her mother. There was only mold creeping up the plastic siding and kudzu threading itself around light posts and clotheslines. There were only drunken men with skimpy mustaches who knocked at the front door on the nights her mother was at work. They said they wanted to help, that a kid her age shouldn't be home alone, but Sid knew she didn't want *their* kind of help.

So Sid walks forward, away from her trailer and her mother, out into the country. The summer sun beats down on her head and she drips sweat. Her throat feels like the floor of Death Valley.

It seems hours ago that she sat on the couch, watching her Saturday morning shows, waiting for her mother to get up and take her to dance class. In reality, it's been only a handful of minutes.

Hoping against hope, she scans the sky for a superhero, coming to her rescue. Why should she be any different than the kids in her shows? Why shouldn't a superhero show up? A GI Joe with a big gun? Superman with his super-strength? Optimus Prime, to scoop her up and drive her to safety?

Her mother said to find help. Maybe she should stop and wait for it instead?

****

Sid stops walking. She is tired, and her leg hurts where Timmy latched onto it. She cries a little, moisture collecting in the crook of her upper lip, and then scans the sky again. It yields nothing more than thick, black columns of smoke, and a handful of vultures circling overhead.

She looks back down, away from the smoke and the ugly black birds, to check the scratch on her leg that is aching and burning.

The sight of her leg makes her cry harder, tears running big and fat and hot down her cheeks. The cut is much bigger, deeper than she expected. The flesh is flaming red and angry, ripped open by what now resembles teeth marks.

Teeth marks? Timmy never bit me before.

Doesn't matter. Mama said to find help, and the superheroes are letting me down.

Sid forces herself to walk again, to break the bindings of self-pity. She tries to ignore the throbbing in her leg, the way the black blood crusts, thick and crackling, all around the wound.

She shields her eyes from the sun for a minute as she trudges forward, and her hand comes away sopping. Her forehead, cheeks, all wet. Her hair curls into damp tendrils that slap her face as she walks. She leaks sweat, her leg burns and her head begins to ache.

Thirst tears at her throat, makes her tongue feel thick in her mouth, and still, there's no help in sight. Just more vultures above.

Sid knows there's a pond further down the road. She's gone there with her mother to look for alligators and throw rocks into the murky water. She heads there now, hoping for a drink.

She tries again to run, thirst a more powerful motivator than fear.

Distracted by the birds above, Sid doesn't see the deep indent in the battered dirt road and she stumbles and falls to the ground with a thud. A cry escapes her parched lips. Though she tries to stifle it, tries to be tough, she can't help but cry. She landed on her bad leg and her face.

Sid pulls herself up, brushing dust from her nose and lips, spitting blood. She takes stock of herself: aching head, busted lip, burning, screaming leg. The leg pain is by far the worst, so Sid dares to look down at it again.

Black lines radiate out from the gash, which is filled with a thick, gray substance. She pokes the flesh beside it and dark green pus squirts out, splattering her other leg.

She jerks her hand away.

The air around Sid is heavy with rot and decay. Something nearby is dead or dying.

That explains the vultures, which swoop lower. She can see them clearly now. They're big, black ones, with feathers like fingers at the tip of each wing. Fingers that could grab her, maim her, hold her down as their razor-sharp beaks tear her apart.

I need to find help, and not just for Mama.

Heart thudding, Sid hauls herself to her feet, but her bad leg feels weak, brittle, like a single step might shatter the bone. Her hands shake and the pounding of her head increases with each step.

Please, Superman. Batman. Spiderman. Someone. Anyone. Rescue me.

Nothing appears on the horizon but more vultures. There are ten now – Sid counts them twice to be sure – swooping and diving through the hazy, smoky sky.

I need to help myself.

Sid hobbles, hopping on her good leg, headed for the pond. She needs a drink to cool her mouth, her head and her leg.

A vulture dives closer.

"Shoo," she says. Her voice is weak and raspy. "Go away. I don't want you."

The bird doesn't land, but neither does he flee.

****

Thirst is hot in Sid's throat. Her body is weak, her hands tremble. Her head swims, her lips crack and blood trickles down her chin.

I just need to get to the pond. To water.

Overhead, the vultures' shadows block the sun and for that Sid is grateful. It's the scent of rot and death that's calling them. Sid can smell it, too. It burns her nose, gags her.

If I don't get to the pond, I'll be the dead, rotting thing calling the vultures.

The realization hits her with absolute certainty.

Sid is too weak to walk, so she begins to crawl. She reaches out, digging her elbows into the dirt to push herself down the road. A newer, sharper pain joins the throbbing ache in her bad leg and she turns to see the opposite side of her calf has burst. Blood, as thick and black as night, spills from the new opening.

Sid would cry, if there were tears left.

There are no superheroes.

She raises her head and pulls, pulls, *pulls* with her arms, off the road and into the grass. She can smell the pond. It's close.

I'm still alive.

She pulls, pulls, *pulls*, crawling on her belly like a soldier, like a GI Joe, and finally she can see it – the pond.

Three more vultures stand on its shore, their wings stretched wide, drying in the sun. They are menacing, terrifying, blocking her way to salvation.

She gathers what strength she has left and cries, "You guys *shoo!*" Her voice is high, piercing, the vultures scatter like ashes, like smoke rising over Sid's trailer park.

She pulls herself across the sand to the cool, thirst-quenching water. Her body quakes and her brain is muddied by clouds and darkness.

She slides down the remainder of the bank.

There, just beneath the water's edge, lays a bloated, rotting hand. The hand is attached to an arm. The arm is attached to a body. The body is dead, headless.

Sid doesn't care. She's not afraid of a dead body. She's not afraid of anything anymore.

She leans in and takes a drink.

****

The sun burns hotter and higher in the sky, coaxing shimmering waves of heat up from the dark dirt road.

Sid lays on the shore, still warm with life but rapidly cooling, even in the heat of the day. Small waves of lukewarm pond water, stirred by a summer's breeze, lap at her head, her hair. Minnows nibble at her fingers.

Thirteen vultures circle overhead.

When minutes pass without Sid moving, they swoop in and land, each with a heavy thud.

The leader approaches.

Taught by a lifetime of close-calls and speeding cars, he is cautious, careful. He hops forward, pokes at her hand, and hops quickly back.

Then, he waits.

Sid doesn't move.

****

"Sid? Sydney? Baby, where are you?"

The voice of Sid's mother is hoarse from shouting. She still wears her see-through t-shirt, though now it is torn across the front, her left breast poking through the hole. If she were to look in a mirror, she would see the trail of blood-red lipstick beside her lips is matched by trails of real blood stretching across her cheek and forehead.

Sid's mother doesn't care about this. All she cares about is finding Sid. Her only child. The unwanted child who destroyed her beauty pageant career.

Her child: the only thing she's ever loved.

"Sid? Syd*ney?* I know you came this way. I see your footprints."

She follows Sid's trail toward the pond.

Please be okay, please be okay, please be okay...

She peers across the tall grasses, and sees the water, steamy in the summer sun. Sweat drips down the side of her face, cutting through layers of day-old makeup and grime, but she doesn't notice.

All she sees are vultures.

"Sid. No."

Her voice is barely a whisper, carried away by the wind.

Three more steps forward and she sees a body in the water. A body that is not Sid's. It's bloated, puffy, and is far too big to be her daughter's. She breathes a sigh of relief.

The area around the pond is a war-zone. Trampled grass, ground stained by blood. All that's missing are more bodies, but Sid's mother can see that whatever happened at her trailer park, has also happened here, leaving nothing behind but the single, headless body floating in the water.

She almost turns around to find another path. One less traveled, less terrifying and disheartening to behold.

She takes another step forward, and there is Sid, face down in the edge of the murk. Her child is surrounded by the heaving, euphoric figures of vultures enjoying their day's meal. She recognizes Sid by the hot pink t-shirt, the purple tu-tu she wore for dance class.

She would not, otherwise, have recognized the torn, bloody carcass before her.

"No!" Sid's mother's voice is a shriek, a howl, and as the vultures take flight, water rains down over the pond from their dripping feathers.

Sid's mother springs forward and falls to the ground, pulling her daughter into her lap. Sand grates against her knees and shins as she cradles the child's wet, slimy head.

Sid's skin, once pink and freckled, is gray and pale. Her body is cold. Entire chunks of flesh have been torn away by the vultures, revealing bloody bone. The smell of decay blankets Sid's mother, and she gags, swallowing back the stomach acids that rise to her throat.

"No," she says again. "Not you. Not my Sid."

Sid is limp in her arms. She doesn't fight her mother's embrace, nor does she return it.

Her mother bends over double, the torn t-shirt fluttering in the breeze. She brings her lips to her daughter's cold, clammy forehead.

Only then does Sid jerk in her arms.

Hope floods Sid's mother's broken heart for a moment. However, hope is a fleeting, inconstant thing.

****

Sid awakens in her mother's arms. Her eyes flutter open, milky and unfocused. Her mouth opens wide, dripping pond water and blood. She nuzzles closer to her mother's neck like a baby seeking a breast.

A sound emerges from her waterlogged vocal chords. It's a low, feral growl.

"Sid?" says her mother, her face beside Sid's cheek. "Baby?"

Her mother tries to pull her head away, to look more closely at the growling thing in her arms, but the child's hand clamps down hard on the back of her neck.

"Sid! Let go! Baby, you're hurting me!"

There are no more words. There is only the fetid scent of pond scum and rotten flesh, and the sound of blood hitting water.

About the Author

Leah Rhyne

Leah grew up on horror, sci-fi, fantasy...you name it, and if it had something scary or nerdy, she loved it. Freddy Kruger haunted her nightmares, while Star Wars filled her daydreams. As a child she had a crush on Mikey, from The Goonies, so her writing tends to reflect those things - a little horror, a little sci-fi, a lot of adventure.

Her first novel, <u>Undead America Volume I: Zombie Days, Campfire Nights</u> released in October, 2012, by MuseItUp Publishing. It's the first of a planned trilogy.

In her spare time, she loves running, punching her punching bag, yoga, and playing fetch with her hound dog.

On the Moors

By Damir Salkovic

The smoking-room of Brooks' was abuzz with conversation, the pitch of voices rising and falling in proportion to the quantity of port previously consumed with a most lavish dinner. Beyond the vast, silk-curtained windows, London had long sank into the confines of night. Yellow fog wreathed the filthy banks of the great river, swallowing the dull gaslight.

"Blasted weather," said Thackeray and swirled the amber liquid in his crystal glass. He turned away from the window. "What is it I hear, we have lost St. Olave? Damned poor showing. Appalling, if you ask me. Pakington should resign, and so should Disraeli, for that matter." He harrumphed and took a large swig. "Any further incompetence and we'll have the Unmentionables shambling around Pall Mall." He punctuated the last sentence by stomping his foot.

His companions made approving noises. "I heard they had to send the dragoons into St Pancras," said a tall, pale young man stretched out on a Turkish divan. He puffed on a pipe, aromatic clouds billowing around his head. "Can you conceive that? St Pancras! Why, that's at the doorstep, so to speak." The young man shook his head in indignation.

"It's quite unlike fighting enemy soldiers," said a portly, red-faced man with a thick mustache and military bearing. "A human foe – no matter from how distant or uncivilized a land – will conduct himself in accordance with tactics, the dictum of strategy. There are logistics to consider, and morale." He halted a tuxedo-clad waiter and retrieved a glass of madeira from the tray in his hand. "Those stricken by the pestilence appear to follow no logic, save the blind, insensate hunger for living flesh. They are but animated cadavers. There is no mind in which to sow the seed of fear, no reason to appeal to, no retreat. It erodes the confidence of our men. One cannot fight an enemy that shows no signs of wearying."

"So, we will all fall victim in the end, Colonel," Thackeray said, his eyes reflexively moving back to the window. The young man barked an uneasy laugh that fell like lead on the sudden silence in the room. "The pestilence has swept the slums and work-houses like a fire, and anyone bitten by the Unmentionables turns into one of them. One by one, until the world is overrun by the damned."

"Babbage would agree with your prediction," the young man said. "His device, this analytical engine, has computed rate of spread of the pestilence on the basis of present reports and the City's records. The results appear to be rather grim."

"Babbage be damned. This is what I think of him and his infernal machine!" The man by the window made an obscene gesture.

"My dear Thackeray!" The portly Colonel guffawed. There was laughter and the conversation in the club resumed, albeit robbed of its previous fervor. Behind the drunkenness and the carousing, behind the devil-may-care air of the upper classes, lurked the spark of mad terror. The curious pestilence that had spread from the fog-ridden, slimy docks of the Thames and the fetid ports of Liverpool and Bristol now held sway over the land. The stricken died in unspeakable agony, only to rise within an hour or two as mindless, shambling cadavers with a hunger for human flesh.

Before the authorities had the opportunity to react, the horror had spread through the filthy, crowded rookeries and dismal dwellings of the poor. The dirty gutters and canals ran red with blood as the dead feasted on the living, those bitten but not torn apart swelling the ranks of the ghouls. The clergy spoke of divine vengeance and called for repentance; medicine was unable to propose an explanation, or provide a cure. The stench of death and corruption mixed with the mephitic vapors of the river.

Panic spread through London as the streets filled with armed soldiers; barricades were hastily erected around the heart of the city to stem the tide of the walking dead. Stories of hordes of Unmentionables roaming the dead cities and plains of the Continent, of darkness descending upon the City of Light and the great fire that consumed Berlin as its inhabitants made a desperate last effort to rid the Prussian capital of the shambling horror, reached the fortified walls.

Yet, the city did not fall. Ships, heavily guarded and closed to all but the soldiers, still navigated the murky waters of the Thames, bringing supplies and news of dead, empty streets of faraway harbors, of the silent wasteland that stretched from the once-bustling ports of Portugal and Spain to the frozen inlets of the north. Passage could still be obtained, at an exorbitant price, on armored trains that rumbled across the island, or on the airships that floated the bleak sky like fat, sluggish predators. Food and spices and even wine, looted from abandoned warehouses in foreign seaports, could still be obtained, albeit at an ever-rising cost. A semblance of normalcy was restored, and were it not for the constant gunfire coming from the fortifications and the persistent reek of rotting flesh, one could close one's eyes and pretend the pestilence never happened.

However, winter was fast approaching, and with it the thick yellow fog; the fog that would limit visibility on the barricades to a handful of paces, taking away the advantage of the long-range rifles of the greenjackets. Murmurs of fear had begun to form among the Londoners. There were places in the Empire where the plague had not yet spread, distant lands of hellish jungles and barren, snow-capped mountains where salvation could be sought. Only the wealthy could afford the journey, and the wealthy refused to leave and thus forswear their place in the social order. What worth was there to life in a desolate back-water, far from Pall Mall and Westminster, from balls and clubs and salons?

"I trust the Army will preserve order," said the young man with a pallid smile. "In time, this dreadful plague will be halted and the stricken cured." He looked to the others for reassurance. The Colonel squared his shoulders.

"No doubt, old boy. In fact, plans are in motion to expand the borders of the perimeter through bombardment of the afflicted quarters from the air. They were ratified by the War Office before…" he cut off abruptly, recalling the grisly scene in the old building in Whitehall; for a moment the madeira threatened to come back up. "Well, never mind; they were ratified."

"We cannot do that," said Thackeray, collapsing into his chair and running his hands through his thinning, pomaded brown curls. Tears streaked down his clean-shaven cheeks. He was very drunk. "There could still be found people in the quarters – living, breathing men, women, small children. Do you propose to murder them all?"

"It is too late to consider that now," said the fourth member of the small circle, a stern, hawk-faced man of middle age seated in an armchair who hadn't spoken a word all evening. He stared into the flames that flickered in the hearth and brought the crystal tumbler to his lips. "We have forsaken the masses. Turned the city into a stockyard for the ghouls to feed on – a stockyard of weak, malnourished cattle, cramped together and defenseless. Betrayed. But the price will be exacted from us, to the last farthing."

"Nonsense, Gladstone," replied the Colonel. "Utter nonsense." He opened his mouth to further refute the speaker, but words failed him; he cast his gaze aside and drained his glass, immediately motioning for another.

"Here comes Wellesley," said the pale youth, eager to relieve the morose hush. "I believe that's the good friend he spoke of at Lady Somerset's a fortnight ago." Two well-dressed men made their way into the smoking-room, throwing their hats and overcoats into the hands of the cloak-room attendant. The taller of the two spotted the group and waved. The young man waved back with a smile. The newcomers made their way through the crowd, stopping briefly to address the waiter.

"Why the somber air, gentlemen?" Wellesley said, flinging himself upon a leather couch. He was a tall, handsome fellow, his hair worn fashionably long and his clothes well-cut; his appearance was marred by a cynical downturn of the mouth and chin. "I trust you won't be terribly perturbed; I have ordered champagne to lighten this dreary mood. Allow me to present to you M. Jean de Chaillet-Volaire, a dear friend of mine, formerly of Paris. He arrived in London by airship, not two hours ago, and I fear his prospects of finding a cold supper are gravely imperiled." His hand swept around the small gathering. "These gentlemen have displayed saintly patience in enduring my scandalous company in the past; they are among the few worthy souls in London who remain both undaunted and uneaten." He proceeded to list their names. The man with him was shorter and stockier of build, dark of hair and eyes where the other was fair. There was a hint of the libertine in his affable, devil-may care appearance. He shook hands with the four men.

"It is a pleasure, gentlemen, to once again travel to London." His voice was even and low, the accent faint. "To walk the streets of a living metropolis, to see lights in the windows, hear song and laughter from the taverns; I had thought those days gone never to return."

"Is the situation in Paris as dire as the papers proclaim?" asked the Colonel.

The Frenchman nodded. "The city was overrun. The soldiers attempted to hold off the cadavres, but they were too few, the bulk of the military having marched on the Prussians. The slaughter lasted for days. I escaped to my father's estate in Picardy at the beginning of the outbreak. Paris is now a tomb, a dwelling of the walking dead. Other cities met with the same fate – Bordeaux, Marseille, Lyon. What is left of the government hides in Toulouse."

"What of the French army?" asked Thackeray.

"Lost," the Frenchman replied. "The plague spread along the battle-lines, taking our men and the Prussians alike. Few returned from the battlefield alive and none with their minds intact."

"Away with melancholy reflections; I hereby decree them forbidden." Wellesley busied himself pouring the champagne, which had just arrived. The men toasted each other's health and drank.

"What brings you to London, M. Volaire?" asked the youth, who had been introduced as Alscott. The Frenchman stole a brief glance at Wellesley, to which the dandy replied with a quick nod of the head.

"I am an avid hunter, Mr. Alscott, and I'm told that the hunting-grounds of England are nonpareil." His dark eyes skirted around the others. "The situation in France does not permit it, but I was told that in England there are secluded, protected parts where a gentleman can indulge this passion – for the correct price, bien sûr."

The men averted their eyes. Gladstone regarded the Frenchman with a wary stare. "There are hunting reserves in the north, Monsieur. A little late in the season, but one can still find grouse on the Yorkshire moors."

"You will forgive me, Monsieur, but I have hardly paid – what is the English expression? – a king's ransom in gold to shoot at game-birds." Volaire smiled, but only with his lips. He emptied his glass and waited for Wellesley to refill it. "I was told that there were other beasts to be hunted on English reserves, if one knew the channels through which such a transaction could be arranged."

Alscott frowned in blank non-comprehension. Thackeray and the Colonel busied themselves with cigars. Wellesley poured champagne all round.

"The hour is late, gentlemen." Gladstone rose stiffly, his stern, patrician visage darkening. "I am to attend a parliamentary session early in the morning. I bid you good-night." The men watched his straight-backed form cut through the chatter and tobacco-smoke and disappear through the door. M. Volaire raised a quizzical eyebrow.

"Do not mind Gladstone," Wellesley said with a wry grin. "Many of our prominent men hold provincial views on the matter, but I assure you it's quite in keeping with the law."

"What on earth does this mean?" asked Alscott, taking nervous puffs of his pipe. Thackeray shot a baleful look at Wellesley, who appeared rather amused.

"You know better than that, Wellesley," the Colonel admonished in a gruff tone. "The old drudge is quite capable of raising a scandal."

"Apologies," the dandy replied, unapologetic. "I see we have upset young Alscott; while your presence delights me, Alscott, I would encourage you to take a stroll around the premises, lest you damage your reputation through talk of wickedness and iniquity." He waited for the baffled youth to leave before continuing. "M. Volaire wishes to accompany us on our hunting expedition. He has generously agreed to cover all the expenses, provided that we make the arrangements." The Frenchman nodded languidly and lit a small, brown, vile-smelling cigar.

"You understand that the cost is considerable," Thackeray said. Volaire waved his comment away.

"Monsieur, any amount seems trifling after purchasing airship fare to London; I am the first Frenchman to have done so without reaching into the pocket of the dwindling Trésor Public. Whatever the price, I am prepared to pay it."

"Then we're on, by Jove." The Colonel's ruddy face lit up with a strange light. "Wellesley and I can pay a visit to Whitechapel tonight. I'll tell my most trusted men to prepare. But Thackeray, you seem to have misgivings; have you lost your nerve?"

"I can't help but think of poor Greyscombe." Thackeray's hands trembled at the recollection; spilled champagne soaked his cuff. "He was bitten during a hunt, by a small child that had crawled through the brush unseen. Shot in the head like a dog, apparently by his own footman. Ghastly way to go."

"That dullard." Wellesley lighted a cigar. "It seems as if the Unmentionables don't abhor the mealy taste of mediocrity." This elicited a round of laughter from M. Volaire and the Colonel. Thackeray seemed to cheer up a little. Another bottle of champagne arrived and Wellesley called for a toast to the Queen.

"It's settled, then," said the Colonel, suppressing a hiccup. "I can have the armored coach ready in minutes."

****

The filthy tenements of Whitechapel rose like dark, sinister islands from a sea of oily mist. Dull gas-light cast long shadows on the walls of the crooked old houses that leaned into one another, rotten from chimney to cellar. The armored car clattered through vacant streets, past heaps of refuse and rubble and pestilent gutters, past the decaying forms of dead men and animals. The coachman and the armed guards who sat on the outside covered their noses and mouths with mentholated liniment to keep out the indescribable stench. The coach-horses were of a special breed, trained to endure the smell of death; even so they cried and bucked, unwilling to descend down certain poorly lit alleys. Whitechapel was a borderland; all but abandoned by the Parliament, it had its own government and laws, slumlords who could afford to keep private militias of hooligans and criminals and who controlled the commerce of supplies through well-established, unseen networks.

The coach halted at a heavy gate of wrought iron, topped with rusted spikes. Four rough-looking men armed with new Martini-Henry breech-loading carbines stood in the stone courtyard; they recognized the crest on the door and opened the gate. Behind them loomed the great, forbidding walls of the poorhouse, blackened with soot and patched with crude, tar-smeared timbers.

As soon as the gate had closed, screaming on rusted iron hinges, Wellesley and the Colonel emerged from the coach, their nose-covers clamped tight to their faces. They hurried up the stone steps and through a side door that had opened, letting out the faint light of an oil-lamp. Inside the stale air stank of damp and squalor, but they breathed it as deeply as the sweetest fragrance. Without speaking a word, they followed a ragged, grim-visaged servant down a spiraling staircase. From below came a dull, repetitive noise, flesh and bone striking wood.

A stout, broad-shouldered man with a face like a slab of pale granite stood in the corridor at the bottom of the stairs. He was clad in ill-fitting evening dress, waistcoat stretched taut over a bulging belly and a dark green velvet coat, from the pocket of which protruded a thick golden watch-chain. He bared his rotting teeth in a grin that called to mind a large, malignant toad.

"Pleasure to 'ave you, milords." He dipped his head in a bow, his small, swinish eyes running over the arrivals. A dusty bottle and several glasses stood on a small table to his left. "Care for a dram? No? To bizness, then." The passage behind his ample back was lined with wooden doors, and it was from behind these doors that the dull sound came, maddening in its monotony; it was followed by a low murmur. The Colonel blanched, but Wellesley smiled back.

"How goes the business, Hayes?"

"Pitifully." The heavy jowls were a picture of despondency; combined with what Wellesley knew of the man's foul reputation, it was all he could do to suppress a laugh. "Not a farthing from the parish in a fortnight, milord, an' a 'undred mouths to feed."

Barnaby Hayes was the Master of the last poorhouse in London, the home to some hundred orphans and indigent poor. Before the outbreak, he was said to own one-third of Whitechapel; under the provisions of the Poor Law he received four shillings for each child and pauper in his care, of which he secreted half into his own pockets.

Yet, somehow his wards were seldom fed the stale bread and watery gruel that was the staple of diet in other poorhouses; they ate vegetables and barley and wheat and received double the required allotment of meat. Hayes was a man of not-inconsiderable ingenuity, a quality that had caught the nobleman's eye long before the plague.

"Perhaps we can relieve your discomfort." The coins in Wellesley's pocket clinked together. Hayes' ears perked up at the sound like those of a good hunting-dog. "We'll pay the old price – an even dozen, two guineas per brace."

Hayes regarded them through slitted eyes, weighing his chances, his hands thrust deep into his coat-pockets. "Can't offer yer the same price as las' time, I'm afeared. Not wi' the costs bein' as they is, an' the bleedin' parish sendin a pair of coves a-sniffin aroun' me ledgers. Three guineas fer each brace, an' yer 'ave yerself a deal."

"Two and three shillings," countered Wellesley, more for the sake of haggling than to spare M. Volaire's coin-purse. The stout man pondered this for a moment. "Two and 'arf, milord, and I'll let yer 'ave 'em on credit. I know yer word is as good as gold."

"That's plain robbery," the Colonel said, flustered. Hayes shrugged his shoulders.

"Plenty of 'em to be 'ad on the barricades, guvnor, at no cost at all."

"Two and five shillings, then." Wellesley counted the coins and handed them over. "Delivered to the same location, four days from now." He watched the man's fat, pale fingers turn the coins over and was seized by a sudden wave of loathing for the bloated creature.

Barnaby Hayes had devised a way by which to rid himself of the most feeble and frail among his wards and turn a considerable profit from the operation. The wretches were taken to the vaulted cellar and fed, screaming and clawing, to the Unmentionables he kept behind lock and key. Once the incubatory period had run its course and the paupers had risen as walking cadavers, he sold them to the wealthy who hunted them in guarded game preserves for sport. It was the new favored pastime of the idle rich: the definitive moral taboo abolished, man hunting man as game.

Hayes swore he only sold those close to death from hunger and disease, whose care would place further strain on the already meager poor rates and deny bread to his hundred hungry mouths. If word got out he would hang for murder; but he had customers in high places, and they knew how to keep mum. When questioned by officials, he purported that the cadavers were captured in the streets of the afflicted quarters, an assertion few attempted to dispute.

Voices in the Parliament cried for the hunt to be outlawed, but were drowned out by those claiming the endeavor to be in the interest of the State. It was not man-slaughter, the apologists proclaimed, for the stricken were already dead, and furthermore posed a peril to the living. The Church condemned cadaver-hunting, and the Queen had decreed it "a base, detestable sport, unfit for gentlemen".

Yet no other deed, no matter how licentious and depraved, could so drug the senses with the heady poison of utter abandon. In the sights of a hunting-rifle, the Unmentionables ceased to be walking dead; the merest squint of the eyes turned them back into men and women and children, slow-moving game to be shot for sport. The very thought of killing without repercussion sent a shiver of pleasure up Wellesley's spine. The new world needed men like Barnaby Hayes, diligent, corrupt creatures crawling through the uncharted darkness of the human soul, working loose the fetters of morality and decency in which the spirit was bound.

"Pleasure doin' bizness wit you, milord." The Master's eyes burned into Wellesley's until the latter was struck by the unpleasant notion that the fat man was reading his thoughts. "Four days it'll be."

****

Remnants of the night's mist trailed across the ground as they stepped out into the chill, damp air of the dawn. A pale radiance in the east heralded the arrival of the new day. The four men stood outside the barred gate of the hunting-lodge, clad in hunting tweeds with tall leather boots. The Colonel and Thackeray had brought their footmen, who lingered in the background, armed to the teeth.

The lodge was built on a small rising, the gray-lit landscape below fringed by thick stone walls. There was a small copse of trees, a pond with reeds and, further in the mist, a hedgerow trimmed to form a labyrinth; all man-made and crafted to enhance the thrill of the hunt. Hayes' ghastly shipment had arrived yesterday and already traversed the grounds. It would be a splendid· day for a hunt, once the mist lifted and the winter sun shone upon the moor.

Wellesley took a deep breath, feeling well-rested and vigorous after a good night's sleep and a light breakfast. He chambered a brass cartridge into his Snider-Enfield and checked his sidearm, an American-made Navy Colt revolver. At his side, M. Volaire sighted down the barrel of his Chassepot rifle; the Frenchman's dark eyes shone with excitement at the prospect of such exotic quarry. The Colonel, who prided himself upon being a crack shot, had opted for a Sharps M1864, while Thackeray, who seldom shot anything, carried a decrepit Needham gun. They hunted without dogs; the animals were too easy a prey for the Unmentionables and the smell of decay was easily picked up by human senses.

The small party made their way down the rise. It didn't take long to spot their quarry; two cadavers soon came into view, wading through the shallows of the pond, apparently baffled by the water. The Colonel's lip curled in distaste: both Unmentionables were crippled and frail, their movements slow and stiff, as if worked by poorly oiled machinery. One of the cadavers was missing an arm, the bloodless stump blackened by gangrene.

"Damn that abominable toad," he said, his voice barely above a growl. "The price gets dearer and dearer, and he sends us rubbish."

"Send your man to bait them into the trees," said Wellesley, inclining his head at the Colonel's valet.

"Hardly worth the trouble." The older man shook his head. "I say, Monsieur, I'll wager ten pounds on my rifle against that old fowling-piece of yours. Mine is on the left. What say you to that?"

"You're on, mon vieux," replied the Frenchman with a genial smile. Wellesley threw his head back and laughed. The Colonel brought the stock of the rifle to his shoulder and leveled the sights. A flock of crows rose from the copse as the shot rang out, a ripple on the still surface of morning.

About the Author

Damir Salkovic

Damir is an aficionado of weird and macabre tales, presently residing in Arlington, Virginia. His interests range from horror and fantasy to science fiction. His stories have been featured in *Tales of the Zombie Wars*, *Tales to Terrify and Schlock Webzine*. He earns his living as an accountant, a profession that lends itself well to nightmares and harrowing visions.

In Loving Memory

By James Gardner

She's eating them potato chips again, Judd Bunton thought, holding a hand over his mouth. It was all his wife Betty did now. She just stared at the glowing television screen, shoveling handfuls of barbecue potato chips into her mouth. Chips would spill down the front of her t-shirt and her mouth reminded Judd of what cows do to their cud. Gobs of just-chewed chips would spill from her maw in orange clumps that wetly stuck to her sweatpants and the couch. This was especially a problem when she heard people laughing on television because she would try to laugh along with them and her jaw would hang open like it was ready to pop off her decomposing face. One long *huuuuuh*, then another and another. Sounding like an asthmatic in the middle of an attack or someone having a really bad shit.

Judd was at least thankful for the aluminum foil over the windows, the only light in the room coming from the television set where Drew Carey looked in danger of being knocked on his bony ass by a happy contestant. The white light of the television made her skin look ghostly, but it covered up some of the greenish tint (like day old lettuce) it had accumulated. Her teeth and gums gathered more shadows day after day, rotting like the rest of her. Her bald scalp, a leftover of the chemo, had skin coming away in places and had spots that reminded Judd of bruised melons at the supermarket.

His nose wrinkled as he caught a whiff of her putrescence. Emptying nearly a whole can of potpourri air freshener over her, Judd wondered if she ever realized how bad she smelled or that she was supposed to be dead. Did she realize that she was moving and chewing on potato chips without needing to breathe? Judd wondered if she remembered him, their first kiss where he played with her red, curly hair, their wedding where she looked so beautiful in her wedding dress and he was so scared and uncomfortable in his tux.

He himself remembered when he thought her wasting away from cancer, becoming a layer of skin stretched over a skeleton, was the worst that could happen. Before being dead was only a temporary condition.

"Betty?" She turned in the direction of his voice, the way dogs do when called. "Time to go to your room, dear." She only looked at him and shoveled another handful of potato chips into her open mouth.

It was a daily ritual, chaining his wife to the hospital bed whenever he had to leave or when he went to bed. Couldn't let any of the neighbors see what his wife had become and she was still his wife. He had gotten a thick industrial chain, the kind his neighbor used to keep his pit bull in check and a dog collar that could circle a Great Dane's neck if need be. In the trailer's spare room, the room where she was supposed to die, sat her hospital bed. At night, baseball bat in hand, Judd would pull the chain on his wife's collar, drag her to the spare room and' chain her to the bed. When he was awake and didn't have to work, he would unfasten the chain with the hand not holding the ball bat and drag his wife to the living room and plop her down in front of the television. In her current state, it seemed cruel to just leave her there to howl by herself.

"Uuuhhhhh!"

"C'mon dear. Let's not make this hard on any of us, okay?"

His wife kicked up a fuss when he started yanking on that chain, clawing for him as she was nearly pulled off her feet. The putrescent stench of her sat in his nose and throat like poured lead. He practically dragged her hundred pound body through the hall like a sack of dry cement and whipped it into the corner. He immediately went to work on fastening the chain.

His wife was crawling toward him seconds after she thudded against the wall and lumbered toward him like some drunk prehistoric creature. She cried out, clawed at him like an old tabby swatting at a fly.

Judd kicked at her, his work-boot connecting solidly on her

chest and launching her across the room. "Sonuvabitch," he muttered, realizing he didn't bring the bat with him, not that he ever used it on her. He couldn't bear to use it on her. It would have, however, made him more relaxed to know it was there and it would have kept his hands from shaking as he tried to fasten the chain.

Just another second, Judd thought. Time moved like molasses in the dingy room. Just a few more—

The padlock clicked shut. He tripped over his own feet. The fall seemed to last minutes rather than seconds. When he hit the floor, he started to crab walk (crab **run**, actually) toward the door. Where his leg had been seconds before, his wife's leering dead face snarled, her jaws snapping shut on empty air and not the meat of his calf.

How many times had he left her and counted his fingers? How many times had he checked his back for scratches at night? Or looked into his eyes in case she was contagious like in the movies? He used to laugh when he and his cousin Dell watched those movies on Saturday nights, Dell drunk and howling about "they's coming' to get ya', Barbara Ann" until someone yelled for them to shut up. Now, thinking about those movies made him sick.

"I'll be back later, hon. Take care." He shut the door as gingerly as a father closes the door to his sleeping child's room. Then, he slid the dead-bolt.

He kept her there for her own good. He couldn't risk letting her wander out and attack anyone, even if their closest "neighbors" were a few miles away. She was clawing at the walls and moaning. He thought about the gun, the .38 he had in his night-stand. They all said, the movies and the scientists, you destroyed the brain and the body dies. However, he simply pulled his keys out of his pocket and headed out the door. Sleep in the bed you made, his mother told him. That's the way life is.

* * * *

Judd hadn't been into Harry's Hardware since Betty died. He

183

sometimes told himself at night that it was out of respect for his wife. But actually outside the place, with its denture perfect cartoon repairman painted on the window, he knew it was to avoid having to talk to *her*.

Unfortunately, he needed the lime. He needed something to stop Betty from reeking and he was getting looks from the women at the Dollar General for buying all their air freshener.

Judd took a breath. A man in a t-shirt and overalls was leaving the store with bags in hands and the tiny, little bell rang, signaling his departure. Taking advantage of the opportunity, he slipped into the store before it closed. He saw a few people milling about, jawing about the weather or politics or who was trying to fix what around the house. He was grateful no one took a notice of him and he began to make a beeline for the bags of lime.

"Hey, Judd."

It was a tiny whisper of a woman's voice as though the voice's owner was afraid to stir the air with words. But it stuck Judd's feet to the floor and, at the same time, stole some of the breath from his lungs, but not enough to steal a response from his mouth.

Without turning, he said, "Frannie."

"I was going to call you, see how your wife was doing. They're still praying for her, you know."

It was amazing how everyone thought that Betty was still among the living, even though they all knew how the cancer ravaged her. Judd didn't even have time to call the Police before Betty rose screaming and scared the shit out of him.

He swallowed, something clicked in his throat. "Yeah, I know."

"How you both holding up? I mean nobody's hardly seen you around."

He felt a tightness in his chest, his back rigid as a rail. "Pretty good considering."

His eyes drifted toward a wheelbarrow painted a fire engine red. He pretended to look at it like he was considering purchasing it, though the wheelbarrow he had at home worked just fine.

"You can turn and look at me, Judd. Promise you won't turn into a pillar of salt or nothing." Frannie laughed to break the tension that engulfed the two of them like morning fog. He felt his shoulders and body rotate, his feet moving to turn his body around. God help me, he thought, I really do want to look at her.

The Harry's Hardware apron did little to hide the curves of her body, hourglass curves that contrasted to his wife's thin frame. She still had the dusting of freckles across her nose and the brown hair swept back in a ponytail she liked to wear, both made her look even younger. Her green eyes looked at Judd, expecting something.

"We can talk, Judd. That's all, just talk." She said this like she was talking him down from a ledge. "We can go out for coffee or something."

"I can't," Judd said. "I just can't."

"Was it that bad between us?" She reached for him. "Was it so wrong what we did?" He noticed she was wearing the same pink nail polish she wore when they first consummated their affair in the darkness of her house. The lovemaking was so eager, like they both would die without the other. All these memories came the instant he looked at her hand. He pulled his hand away, rubbing at where she touched him.

"I have to go," he muttered and was walking quickly, nearly running, to the exit.

"You're still alive," she yelled after him and Judd wanted to crawl into a hole and pull the dirt in after him. "You're still human, Judd Bunton."

Judd left Harry's Hardware like he was being followed, but there was no one. Only when he finally got himself in his truck did he feel secure. He looked at the people coming in and going out of the store, looking at him like he just robbed the place. He wanted to scream at them to go fuck themselves, but yelling wasn't in his nature.

He fumbled with his keys and missed the ignition once before finally starting it up. He needed to drive somewhere, somewhere where no one could see him.

* * * *

Just shoot in the morphine. Find the vein and shoot in the morphine. That was his plan. His poor Betty would no longer suffer, just float away on a drug-induced dream. "She needed the peace, Lord," Judd said aloud in his truck as it sat parked outside the church. "Dammit, she needed the peace." He didn't care about jail. He just cared about his wife and he'd tell any jury that he couldn't understand why she had to keep suffering.

Within his truck, he sat looking at the Freewill Baptist Church he and his wife faithfully attended for years, where he spent hours talking to God and asking him questions. How many times did he come here and pray? How many times did he lower his head reverently and whisper his prayers to God, not caring who heard them? How many times did he come to church in a suit that was getting a little tight around his middle and ask the Lord for guidance? Why would God do this to him? At least when Job's family died, they didn't come back as . . .

Judd didn't even want to think the word. The fact that she came back as something from movies he used to laugh at seemed more and more like a sick joke. He remembered laughing at those movies, where the dead were just actors with make-up smeared on their faces and shadows painted under their eyes. They weren't funny when the skin of someone you love and cherish gangrenes and peels off like old latex paint or starts to smell so bad he was tempted to open a window no matter who might see. They weren't funny when someone you shared a bed and your heart with can now only laugh at the television, stuff potato chips in her mouth without eating them, and try to take a hunk out of your arm when your mind's drifting to the way things were.

He thought back to Frannie, their one night of bliss, his one night of weakness. She was full and ripe with womanhood and wanting. He was just in need of forgetting he was married and his wife was dying. He remembered Frannie's hair smelled like strawberries and it felt good just to give in, to let the mask of the caring, stoic husband slip. Frannie, who wanted only to heal his broken spirit, tempted Judd with her doe eyes and soft body. Judd had bitten the apple and goddamn if it was delicious.

Judd looked up at the corner of his windshield where the sun was trying to peek through the steel gray clouds, where as a boy he imagined God watched over his life. He wondered if it was that night that brought Betty back. Governments and scientists were looking at bodies in space or chemicals in the air. What if this phenomenon was because men like Judd Bunton, thirty-four years old and a humble roofer, finally cheated on their wives too much or secretly wished they were dead? Instead of radiation or pesticides, God may simply be getting more creative in the way he smites.

He saw over the horizon the black plume of smoke rising into the sky. The incinerator has been running more and more frequently as more dead had been spotted and dispatched. It was like the movies: how much longer before the dead outnumbered the living?

Judd suddenly saw Reverend Royce stepping out of the rectory in sweats, dusting his hands as though he was ready to do some work. Judd ducked down to avoid being seen by the Reverend, to avoid conversations about God or his wife. He started up his truck.

He needed answers, but Judd Bunton, thirty-four years old, roofer, and possible walking target of the Almighty's wrath, decided to dull his need for answers with alcohol.

* * * *

Frannie wasn't sure why she was here. She had even asked her Daddy for time off, telling him she wasn't feeling too well and batting her eyelashes. She just stood at his doorway where his wife was probably resting, maybe even sleeping and here she was ready to disturb her. A pang of guilt stabbed at her throat. Plus, she desperately wanted to see Judd again.

She pulled her sweater tighter against her arms to help ward off this unusual chill for April. The sky was a uniform tombstone gray, threatening rain. She could actually smell the rain coming and knew it would feel like ice on bare skin.

Frannie wondered what she hoped to accomplish here. Surely, telling her about her and Judd's tryst would not be good for a woman who was close to dying. Shouldn't she just leave the poor woman alone to die with her faith in her husband intact?

However, the guilt was eating at her. The night with Judd felt good. Strong and sensitive, he had played her body like a fine instrument, but he was married and he still loved his wife, had said so as he put his clothes back on so he could go back and check on her. Truth is, she was here now because she wanted to see the woman who had so stolen the heart of the man she loved.

Frannie saw Judd like those heroes on the covers of the romance novels she picked up from the drug store. The hard lines and angles of his chest visible through his T-shirt, the soft blue eyes and chiseled jaw most actors would kill to have.

She also liked to heal things. Her Daddy complained about how she was always bringing strays home, but she couldn't leave them with broken legs, starving bellies or emotional scars caused by disturbed people. She even applied to MSU's Nursing program so she could help stop others from hurting. Judd was hurting, his body practically hummed with anxiety. He deserved to be healed.

Thwam!

Pulled out of her thoughts, her head swept left to right, trying to find the source of the noise. Whatever the noise was sounded close.

Thwam!

It sounded like it was coming from inside the trailer, like someone banging on a window. Not a heavy rap-rap-rap like she expected, like the way her mother used to call her in to supper when she was a girl.

Looking at the windows, Frannie noticed that the windows were covered with foil, thought it odd. She wondered if something about her cancer made Judd's wife light sensitive or was she simply demanding that Judd makes sure no one sees her.

Thwam!

Frannie pictured Betty falling out of bed, or maybe in need of some medication that she couldn't get herself. She pictured Betty in her hospital gown a few feet from the window. "Hello?" she called. "Mrs. Bunton, can you hear me?" She knocked furiously on the door.

After a while, there was the twitter of a blue jay and the putter of a tractor, but nothing coming from inside.

She checked underneath the large welcome mat where she hoped Judd hadn't checked recently. She picked up the same house key she knew about from when she made deliveries here. She told herself she'll just pop in and tell Mrs. Bunton she thought she fell down and wanted to see if she's okay, ask her if she needs anything.

Frannie opened the door and felt something catch in her throat when the smell hit her. It was a chemical smell, overpowering, but still not powerful enough to cover the earthy smell underneath, the smell of fresh dirt and bad meat.

Inside the trailer, the smell was stifling and seemed to be taking up space in her lungs, filling them to the point of bursting. She remembered this smell from when she was ten. Her favorite cat Whiskers disappeared for weeks, only to be discovered when she and her Mamaw were putting up canned tomatoes in the cellar. Whiskers was there, quite dead, eaten away in places by hungry maggots. The smell of poor Whiskers filled the cellar to the point that, even if it was Mamaw's delicious canned preserves, she couldn't stand to think of eating anything that was stored in there.

The darkness from the covered up windows only added to the claustrophobia that sent her heart fluttering. She swatted at the wall, desperately looking for a light switch. Panic made her legs tighten like an animal ready to spring. She was a second away from sprinting out of this trailer and into the slightly cool, but natural air outside. The lights came on and her panic subsided. Only to be replaced by disgust.

Frannie saw the potato chip crumbs littering the floor and piles of them like sawdust could be found on the couch cushions. Aerosol cans were stacked on the kitchen table like bowling pins. When she looked closer, there was can after can of Lysol in scents ranging from Potpourri to Mountain Fresh. She picked one up and shook it, hearing the telltale rattle, but when she sprayed she discovered it was empty. It seemed obvious to Frannie that Judd wasn't the best housekeeper. *What could smell so bad?* The combination of the overuse of Lysol and whatever reek the Lysol was supposed to cover was making her nauseous.

"UHHHHHHHH!"

Frannie screamed and knocked over the cans where they clattered hollowly on the kitchen floor. She backed into the counter and put her hand to her rather abundant chest where her heart thumped like a boxer's speed bag.

"Hello?" she called out. "Are you okay, Mrs. Bunton?"

"HUUUUUUU--" she heard and she thought that whoever it was, was choking. But the voice suddenly changed to "LOOOOOOOO." She was saying "Hello." The realization chilled Frannie. She wondered how much of Judd's poor wife was left. Frannie wondered what kind of cancer was eating away at the poor woman.

Frannie knew there was something seriously wrong, that Betty Bunton was in pain, that maybe Judd was neglecting her, left her in her bed wallowing in her own filth with her only recourse to cry out for help.

"HUUUULOOOO!"

Now, it was more like an animal bark. She wanted out of here. She could call the Police **and** some paramedics. Judd might be home any minute. What the Hell did he do to her?

"HUUUULP MUUUEEEE."

"Hello?" she called out, looking for a fix on where it was. After all, it was a trailer. How many rooms could it have?

"HUUUUUUULOOOOOOO?" Mrs. Bunton called out. It sounded like it was coming from down the hall. Frannie walked steadily down the hall, her can of pepper spray in hand. She realized she should be running toward the source of the shouting, but her feet didn't respond. Frannie felt in some primitive part of her mind that something in this trailer was waiting to grab her, perhaps it was Judd himself so he could keep his dirty, little secret quiet.

"Tell me where you are," Frannie called out.

"WUUUUUUHEEEEEER," she replied.

Then she heard it, scratches on the door. She saw the dead bolt on the door and was aghast. She pulled it back. She slowly opened the door, listening for Judd. Judd Bunton, she thought, you deserve to burn in Hell for this.

"FRANNIE NO!"

Hearing Judd's voice she backed into the room. Something pounced on her shoulders. She heard her sweater tear, then immediately felt part of herself tear away. Something warm and thick was flowing down the front of her sweater, darkening it to the color of dead rose petals.

She tumbled forward and reached for the door, twisting her body to try and throw whatever it was off, but it clung tightly, clawed fingers digging into her skin for purchase. The floor seemed to spin and flip like a carnival ride even as the colors seemed to bleed out of it. The door to the hall might as well have been a hundred yards away.

Then. a pair of booted feet thudded into view, a voice called out to "GET OFF HER!" Whatever it was did, but only after a meaty thwack, then another. Strong hands pulled her into the hall. She turned and saw whatever it was reaching for her feet, a deathly face straight out of a nightmare, mouth stretching wide as skeletal fingers clawed at her feet. All Frannie could do was mutter "I'm sorry" to Betty Bunton's snarling, twisted face over and over again.

* * * *

It happened so fast Judd wasn't sure he had actually pulled

Frannie away until he had put her on the couch. His wife moaned, perhaps upset that her meal had escaped, while said meal's neck gushed blood like rainwater through a gutter, making the dark stain on her sweater grow wider with each passing second.

The seconds seemed to be moving fast and Judd felt like he was on a roller coaster in danger of leaving the tracks. He quickly ran a dishrag under the faucet. He screamed to Frannie to hold it against her neck. Frannie's eyes seemed to be gazing through the ceiling but she complied. Soon, the rag was dark and heavy with blood.

"Don't die, Frannie." He whispered. "Don't you die too."

Betty moaned from down the hall as though she were dying all over again. The chain rattled as she attempted to pull free.

"SHUT UP YOU BITCH!"

His yelling made him feel low and horrible, like a true monster. Yelling at her like that was an ice pick in his heart.

Why does Frannie have to pay? He thought. She has a life ahead of her, Goddamn. It was the first time he used "God-dammit," even in his thoughts.

Frannie's skin was the color of wet paper mache and she was shivering. Once again, Judd thought back to the movies he'd seen and laughed at while having a few beers. All it took, according to the movies and the scientists, was a bite. A bite and one was doomed to walk the earth with barely an idea of who you were, a walking insult to both that person's life and death.

"Judd," the word was a whisper, like the one she had placed in his ear when they lay together. Only this whisper had little breath behind it. "Judd, I'm cold."

How long before she became like Betty who was wailing and scratching at the carpeting in the hall? Who spent her days letting half-chewed potato chips fall from her mouth and grinning stupidly at Bob Barker? Who spent her days reminding Judd that his Betty, the Betty he took to prom where she wore a purple dress that brought out her eyes, the Betty he made love to who smelled like flowers in rain, the Betty whose smile brought a joyous ache to his heart, was gone forever?

Judd ran to the night-stand where he kept his .38. It was even loaded and ready to fire but it was hard bringing himself to do what he felt he should. He made sure Frannie wouldn't see him, wouldn't ask why. He doubted she'd understand it was to stop the spread of it (Judd wasn't even sure what "it" was). He put the muzzle to the back of her head, wondering if she was growing cold already. When she lifted her head and moaned loudly like he'd heard Betty do a thousand times, he pulled the trigger out of reflex. "I'm sorry," he said. He wanted to tell her he loved her, but he was just sorry she got into this.

He could feel the tightness in his muscles, like they were all trying to pull taut at once. His whole body shook like a plucked guitar string. His skin felt too small for his body, his scalp especially because it constricted his brain. Something dark and ugly was boiling in Judd's soul, he could almost taste it in his mouth. The gun shook in his hand, and there was another bullet he had to fire. A ghastly smile stretched the corners of his mouth, as he quietly repeated the mantra of "my Betty's gone."

He strode down the hall, repeating his mantra, the gun feeling hot and alive in his hand. Betty sat with her arms hanging in her lap, smiling up at Judd and looking at the gun as though it was some kind of present. Frannie's blood was smeared on her face, smeared by its (whatever his wife was now) hands. Betty's grin soon widened, showing all the gaps where her teeth had been. Her eyes seemed clearer now, clarity brought on by meanness, the same smile a boy gives when he pulls the wings off flies or shoots cats with BB guns.

He raised the gun, forcing his shaking hand to aim. He blinked away the tears so he could see the target. "Did you know about us, Betty?" he asked suddenly. "Did you know?"

She just screamed at him, screamed in anger like she would have liked nothing better than to tear him to pieces and watch him bleed. Her eyes looking straight into Judd's as she screamed, her mouth stretching down to her chest as she screamed. She screamed seemingly without needing to breathe and kept screaming until Judd put two in her head and she fell back. She laid still, a crumpled heap of meat and bones. He stood there, no longer shaking but empty and hollow inside now that his anger was spent.

Judd got his chain-saw from the shed. He wanted this done quickly. He carved up the bodies of both women till there were pieces that could fit in a lunch box and even then he noticed that their fingers twitched and writhed like earthworms left on the sidewalk after a rain.

Night had swallowed the trailer and the land it sat on as he worked and even the stars seemed to be hiding. He had just filled up that morning and pumped most of that gas out to use on the trailer. It burned steadily into the night as he drove away from town, away from his life.

He pulled a picture from his pocket. It was Betty wearing a bikini top and shorts out on Cave Run, playfully waving at the camera. Her skin was pale and smooth. Her red hair shone in the sunshine. He tried to compare this picture with the image of the shrieking, hateful thing he had just put down.

It's my old life, he thought. It's rotted away.

Judd thought, as he shoved the picture angrily in his pocket, that God's message, in this new world, was simply that the dead can only hurt.

About the Author

James Gardner

James Gardner is a writer of speculative fiction that reflects his roots in Eastern Kentucky, a land of natural beauty and proud heritage. He graduated from Morehead State University with a Bachelors and Masters in English. James has taught writing and literature in several kinds of schools, from high school to college, and loves to practice what he teaches. He has already been published in online magazines like *The Harrow* and Bluegrass Community and Technical College's *Accolades* as well as anthologies like *Lucha Gore: Scares of the Squared Circle* but strives to show his work to all kinds of readers.

SURVIVORS

By Gary Reed

He never knew her name.

She had told him when they first met but he didn't bother to remember it. He never wanted to know names or get close to anyone in this new world. The old world was gone. Now friends and acquaintances were future enemies even after they died... especially after they died. The living saw what was once life in the blank eyes of the dead and names added to that memory. The dead, they only saw the living with a perverse hunger, nothing more. The memories were gone, replaced with a gnawing for the substance of human flesh Love had died with the memories. He had seen mothers attack daughters, fathers devour wives, and children lay into their infant siblings.

No, he had no desire to remember her name. The monsters had to be nameless...they had to be faceless. And you never knew when a person with a name would become one of the monsters. The safety of anonymity in killing the walking corpses compelled him to keep moving further from his home. He traveled far from his past and pushed the memories out of his head. He dove deep into unknown areas where his old world, his old memories, were securely behind him. He had to keep his focus on how things were, not how they use to be, not how he wished they were. He found a strength in the solitude.

But he knew he was failing. This nameless woman in front of him seared his memory. She was just "the woman" and the deniability of a name didn't limit her presence in his mind. He had been avoiding her because he knew she could pull him in and that was the last thing he wanted in this world.

He looked into her brown eyes. Piercing, they saw deep. They should have been blue. It was supposed to be blue eyes that could break the barriers of pretenses and facades. Brown eyes were full of compassion, of tenderness. Hers were not. They were direct and captivating with no signs of weakness, either in her resolve or emotions.

Her tussled hair hung long in brown strands. There was a certain nobility in its unkeptness. It gave credence to her acceptance of the new world; it gave her the appearance of strength that she needed. Her thin lips showed a firmness that obscured physical size. But when she parted those lips, the pink softness inside of the still white and perfectly straight teeth, exuded her sensual side. She wasn't cute, she wasn't beautiful in the refined sense but she was exotic and exquisite in her naturalness. He knew even in the old days that she was never one of those plastic faces that was built on a foundation of cosmetics. Her essence was always true.

He controlled himself around her. Every time he got close, he could feel a weakness come over him. He would lose himself in her smell, her presence. A lightness came over him as if he were being absorbed into her. It was more than just simple passion; it was a state of surrendering completely to another…to get lost in emotions so strong that it drained the body physically. He couldn't afford that. He couldn't let himself lose touch of his mission of survival. Deep down, he knew he could never handle the pain if it ended, so he stayed detached from her, fighting the impulse to hold her, to caress her, to lose himself in her. Sex was not the driving component, it was the closeness with her that overwhelmed him.

He could sense that she too ignored any feelings. She had learned the hard way of what the allowance of passion and love in this world could bring. Pain. The kind of pain that only comes with a great loss. Tennesseean had said it was better to have loved and lost than never to have loved at all. But that was said in a different time, a different world. They had both decided on their own that in order to avoid the pain, you had to avoid the passion.

He stood in front of her and an awkward silence passed. He knew before that he could take her and she would struggle, not of repulsion or fear, but because she had to. They would both temporarily expel the demons of passions without the commitment of potential pain. It would be a non-binding alliance that would permit each of them safety, a lack of acknowledgment of succumbing to the passion, but he never wanted her that way. He did not want memory of just her body, it was the closeness that he desired.

This time was different, though. She had a wall of seriousness surrounding her and her eyes, blood red from crying, showed no hidden suggestions. She was purposeful and deliberate in her words and her actions. There was a specific agenda she had in mind for this moment and nothing else was to be considered. He stood there silently. It was her resolution and he knew he had to follow her decision, her way. He knew why she asked him to come. He didn't want to do what she was asking him to do, but it was a request of reason. He would not refuse her. It made sense. He knew that she had overcome a great deal of personal agony before approaching him and words and questions were useless between them now. No one would have the right to judge them, not even each other. This was why he was lured towards her and felt the forbidden passion. *She understood.* She accepted what it took to live in this world. Survival was something that no one ever knows if they can deal with until they come up against it. It had nothing to do with bravery, with physical skills or strength, or knowledge. To survive, you just had to do it. Survive. You had to do what had to be done. Everything had a cost but the drive had to go beyond morality, beyond right or wrong. The instinct for survival had to be the single most compelling need. She was a survivor.

He remembered when he first saw her. She came to the cabin with her husband as they fled what was left of civilization. They were like so many who felt safety was in hiding from the world until it settled down. A few months, maybe a year, and then they could return. He had talked to them briefly once and immediately knew how things were going to work out for the couple. The husband was the one who felt things would go back to normal soon, but when he first looked into her eyes, it told him everything.

She knew. She knew that the world had changed forever and that it was time to deal with it. But she allowed her husband's hopes to become hers, and maybe, just maybe, he was right. She also had more important things to worry about. Her husband patted her stomach and pushed the pride of a first time father. In five months, he was going to have a son.

He hid his amazement behind a face of no expression but inside his head, his thoughts were racing. *Why would anyone want to bring a baby into this world?* He guessed that the father wanted to, simply because he could. From the woman, however, he sensed something more. Not only an acceptance of things but perhaps a greater understanding that he had himself. If the humans were to survive, the best way would to bring in those who would deal with the situation from birth. The new ones wouldn't be plagued by memories and wishes of how things used to be. They would be stronger as it wouldn't just be a matter of acceptance, it would be the way of life, the only way of life they knew. Perhaps that would be the key for the continuation of the human race.

The husband treated the situation as a chance to prove himself. He was skilled in all the right areas but he didn't fully understand what was at stake. His attitude was one of a game. By the looks and actions of the husband, he wouldn't last more than a month.

The husband actually managed to survive for six weeks.

He watched as he saw the woman drag her husband's body over to the shallow grave. She had waited until the rains came to make the ground softer. The grave was more circular than the traditional rectangle, after all, it wasn't a casket that contained her husband's body, but a large plastic bag that belied any shape. She had tried to find all the pieces but she knew that many parts were in the bellies of the dead. What happened after that, she didn't care to know.

She worked slow and methodical. She was careful not to over-extend herself, especially in her condition. She would never know how her husband died, how he got caught by the walkers. At first, she was more angry than saddened by his death. Now she was alone and almost ready to deliver a baby by herself because he had gone and got himself killed. Her anger played out and she, like a true survivor, knew she just had to deal with it.

He watched her silently from the shadows of the trees. Even though the burial was an unpleasant detail that he could have helped her with, he felt that she would want to do it herself. It would be an infringement on his part to intrude. Besides, he had done enough already.

He had found the husband walking the dirt path that came up behind the cabin. His chest had been blown open by a shotgun blast, probably from another husband who had fled the city. The hunter had undoubtedly panicked and shot, thinking this man was one of the dead. It was understandable, why take chances?

He saw the meandering walk of the husband and realized what had happened. The body had been partially eaten but when the eyes popped back open, the dead had given up eating him, like a dinner that's gone cold.

He used his machete, first to decapitate the man to spare the woman from seeing her husband as one of the walking dead. Then he hacked the body so it looked like it was tissue torn by dull teeth. No sense in worrying the woman about some scared human running around with a shotgun. The pain of his death was enough-she didn't need more.

He started to visit her often after the burial of the husband. He found himself no longer inventing excuses to stop by and the hours would pass by as they discussed the world, both past and present. She hid the grief of her husband's death well and the topic was never brought up. He admired her intellect and couldn't help smiling as she brought up old songs for every situation. When she laughed, she exuded an angelic radiance. He knew that he was becoming absorbed by her.

He worried about her delivery and promised himself to help... somehow. He was spared. One time, after being away for two days, he heard the cry of the baby as he neared the cabin. She had delivered it herself. It wasn't that aspect that surprised him so much, for it had been done for centuries, it was the sound of the baby. It seemed to be a foreign sound that was not meant for this world. It was a sign that maybe the humans had a chance after all.

She fussed over the baby constantly and read up on all the books she had taken from the library before her trek up here. She thought of nothing else but the baby and if he wasn't there, she probably wouldn't even eat. Although he tried to take care of her, she neither thanked nor acknowledged him. The only time she showed any emotion was when he went near the baby. Then she pushed him away.

He knew what was wrong. It had to be. The baby had died and then returned. The mother wouldn't accept that. But she would have to, no matter what. He had to know so he stormed into the cabin while she was sleeping in the chair. The suddenness of his actions slowed her enough so that he quickly swooped up the baby before she could stop him. He looked to find the dead eyes set back in the pallid skull, a toothless mouth hungrily gnawing at whatever might come its way.

He found neither.

The baby had her brown eyes. His skin was pink and pale, lined with thin blue veins racing through the translucent skin. The mouth opened, not to chew, but to cry. He felt a great relief in that cry.

"I had to know," he said to her as he handed the infant, the live infant, back to her.

She said nothing as she cuddled the baby next to her. She casually undid her top and released a breast and the cry of the baby was replaced by suckling noises.

"You saw?" She said in a whisper without lifting her head.

He nodded. He watched the baby eat greedily and only looked up when he saw the hairless head becoming stained with the tears that dropped from his mother's eyes. She was crying silently.

"He's blind," she stated, "and I'm pretty sure he's deficient... retarded. I checked all the books and all the indications are there. Besides, I can tell."

She sat down and took a deep breath, instantly regaining her composure.

"I kept thinking that maybe it wouldn't be true if I gave him more time. One morning I would come and get him and he would see me. He would respond the way he was supposed to. I just thought maybe...maybe, I could give him more time."

They sat quietly for an hour. She never made any mention of why she had an abnormal baby. She didn't look to place blame anywhere; no questioning pleas to a God who seemingly had already shunned this world; no trauma of self doubt in her prenatal care. It was the way things were, the way things are. She accepted this first and foremost.

He could sense it was time to go. He shouldn't come back for awhile. The world outside no longer existed for her. Her world was wrapped up in a little bundle inside the cabin and he was a reminder that the other world did indeed, exist. He left and stopped coming back. He would cut wood and leave it for her and drop off food supplies but he never came up to the cabin. He still had the rest of the world to deal with.

Now, after four months, she had contacted him by leaving a note on the trail. He had come without knowing why. When he came up to the cabin, she had pointed to the cradle. Then he knew.

"I can't keep watching every day. The love just grows too strong. He's becoming my life and I don't know what's going to happen out there." She talked while keeping her face in the shadows.

He saw the short wave radio on the table and knew that she had been listening as he had been. The situation was becoming worse daily. Few humans seemed to be left. How long could any of them survive?

"I-I don't now how I can ask-", she stammered.

"You don't have to. I understand."

"His name was...is..." she tried to say before he stopped her.

"No, I don't want to know. You can put it on the marker if you want, but I--".

Now, she interrupted him. "I understand."

She stepped towards the open door. Her hand grabbed for support but she quickly steadied herself. "I took care of everything. If you could...you know...I-I'll come back and cover him up.

"I came to you because I know what you did for my husband...for me. I figured you didn't think I knew so I never said anything. I never thanked you for it."

"No need," he said.

She took a step out and raised her face to catch the warm breeze. "You know, even though he never saw me, I'll never forget his face. I'll remember his softness, his dependency. I hope that he stays more than just a memory to me. But I can't bring him into this world, not so disadvantaged. I would rather --- I just can't see him becoming...one of them."

Her hand slipped off the doorway as she stepped fully out. He could see her step in front of the cabin and her hesitation on where she should go...where she could go. She knew it really didn't matter where she went. The ordeal was with her for the rest of her life, another scar on the thickening mass of sacrifices made for survival.

He could see the small open grave through the doorway. Next to the cradle, he saw a couple of blankets that were ready. On top of the blanket, he saw a hatchet that had been freshly sharpened.

He waited until she got out of sight before he picked up a pillow and headed over to the baby's cradle.

About the Author

Gary Reed

Gary Reed is the writer of the Deadworld series which last year had nominations for best mini-series from the Shel Dorf Awards, the Ghastly Awards (winner), and the Comic Monsters Awards. Deadworld's next series comes from IDW in the fall of 2013. Gary Reed has also written Saint Germaine, Raven Chronicles, Renfield, and some additional 20 graphic novels. He is also the publisher of Transfuzion Publishing and Binary Publications and was the former publisher of Caliber Comics and served as Vice President of Todd McFArlane's toy company.

Gary Reed was presented with the Shel Dorf Torch Bearer's Award – "For Preserving the Flame of the Spirit of Comics and Carrying the Torch Forward in the Comic Industry" at the 2012 Shel Dorf Awards.

You can learn more about Gary Reed at:

http:/www.garyreed.net/

You can learn more about Tranfuzion at:

http://www.transfusion.biz

You can learn more about Deadworld at:

http://www.garyreed.net/?Deadworld/home.htm

Printed in Great Britain
by Amazon.co.uk, Ltd.,
Marston Gate.